Tyler Hill's

Decision

Tyler Hill's

Decision

Dannie C Hill

Author- Dannie C Hill

Published by
Small Mountain Publishing
Houston, Texas
http://smallmountainpub.com

Cover and interior design by,
Small Mountain Publishing

Edited by
Sherry Ruschell

First printing in
The United States of America
ISBN-13: 978-0-9826924-0-0

Dedication

To my grandson Tyler Zion Hill

With love and hope for the future.

Acknowledgement

To my wife Julee, whose patience and encouragement has seen me through for many years.

I would like to thank my editor, Sherry Ruschell, for all the hard work and candid comments that makes my work better.

Tyler Hill's Decision

Chapter 1

Tyler Hill lay in his sleeping bag, unable to sleep. It was late and he knew from the sounds around him that everyone else was fast asleep.

He thought, 'This must be what it's like to be blind.'

It was pitch black; he couldn't see his hand in front of his face and he was wide awake. He was excited about the climb up the mountain in the coming morning. This was his first time camping deep in the Appalachian Mountains and he was amazed at how cold it could get at night, even in the summer.

He heard a noise outside his tent. It sounded like a dog sniffing around for food, but it must be a really big dog because the noise was loud and close to his side of the tent. Then he heard grunts and digging close by.

'It must be a bear,' he thought. 'I told Lamar not to bury the leftover food so close to the tent,' but Lamar, Tyler's best friend, wanted to see some bears. 'Well, here's his big chance.'

He reached out and shook Lamar's sleeping bag and all he got was a grumble and blowing noise out of Lamar. The grunts and sniffing noise stopped outside as Lamar groaned.

'That wasn't a good idea,' he thought.

Slowly the noise started up again, but now it was moving towards the flap opening in the front of the tent. Tyler reached for his pack that held, among other things, his flashlight. He pulled the bag inside his sleeping bag. He grasped the flashlight and pointed it towards the front of the tent and slid the switch forward. It was a really nice flashlight with brand new batteries and the light shot out like a laser beam that blinded him for a moment.

He closed his eyes against the brightness and when he opened them again he was looking into the face of a big black bear. Its nose was wet and shiny black and it had beady little eyes set back from a long snout. The bear's fur was glossy black and its body more than filled the entrance to the tent.

The beam of light must have startled the bear because it rose up on its hind legs, opened his muzzle and roared in what Tyler hoped was fright. All Tyler could see now were four giant fangs as the bear roared again.

When it roared it must have startled the other bears that were searching for food because one of them slapped and bit into the roaring bear's rear end. The bear, standing inside or really standing with the tent wrapped around it, made a yelping sound of fright at being bitten and having the nylon tent wrapping itself around him. It leaped forward and Tyler rolled to the side as best he could while still inside his sleeping bag. The ground shook where the bear's paws slammed into the earth next to Tyler's head as it ran off with the tent wrapped around its head.

Tyler turned the beam of the flashlight towards the direction the bear had taken and it was almost comical to see the beast slamming into trees and bushes as it ran blindly through the forest. It hit a larger pine tree that did not yield to its great power and the bear fell to the ground but then it leaped back up to continue its blind rampage through the forest.

Tyler turned the beam back and now he was looking at not one but two big bears and, to his consternation, they were looking at him. He tried to remember all the instructions the scout leader had given to the boys about what to do if they came across a bear. Don't look directly at them and back away very slowly until they lost interest. Good advice, he guessed, except he was stuck inside his mummy-style sleeping bag and the two bears didn't seem to be losing interest. They were both sniffing the air and one lowered its head toward Tyler's feet. Tyler rose up just enough to look at the bottom of his sleeping bag and saw that someone had rubbed peanut butter all over the bottom of it. At that point he ducked into his bag, curled up into a ball and turned the light off.

By now the boys were waking up in the other tents around the camp and flashlights were shooting white laser beams into the night.

There were shouts and screams and someone was yelling, "Bears!"

At the same time the others were beginning to panic the first bear had run in a circle and was heading back into the camp with the tent firmly wrapped around its head. It ran straight through another tent and it too wrapped around the bear and tangled its feet. It tumbled to the ground.

There were screams and people fleeing all around but finally one of the leaders, who had brought a large pistol with him, drew the pistol and fired two loud shots into the air.

Everyone froze except the three bears. The one wearing two tents sprang forward with great speed and ran directly into the trunk of a giant pine tree. It hit so hard it must have knocked itself out because with a muffled grunt it hit the ground and lay still.

The other two bears were busy trying to lap up the peanut butter and were paying no attention to the screams and shouts until the pistol went off. When it roared out, with fire leaping from the barrel, the larger of the two bears snatched up the end of Tyler's sleeping bag and leaped forward with it dragging along beside him. The other bear, having tasted the excellent brand of peanut butter, was not about to let it get away so it was right behind the other bear, trying to take a bite out of Tyler's sleeping bag.

Chapter 2

Tyler hadn't seen anything after he ducked inside his bag, but the noise of screaming and yelling and the fact that the two bears were chewing on the end of his sleeping bag made him curl even tighter. When the pistol went off he jerked in fright and then he was moving at what seemed to be great speed. He reached up to the small opening in his sleeping bag and got his hand on the edge of the hole. He was trying to unzip the bag but at the same time he was bouncing and scraping though thick bramble and small trees. He reached out as far as he could and grabbed a handful of thick fur and realized that it was the bears that had him. He had hoped some of his buddies had grabbed his bag and were pulling him away from the bears.

Just as he was going to let go of the thick fur his bag hit a small tree and it lifted into the air and swung onto the back of the bear. Tyler got his other hand out of the bag and grabbed another handful of fur. The ride was much smoother than crashing through bushes and trees. It was like riding a crazy roller coaster backwards. His feet were forward and his head was toward the tail of the bear. He could smell the powerful odor of the bear and it caused him to gag. It was the smell of dead things, dirt, leaves and a musky smell that reminded him of the tigers at the zoo. He was frightened but he had to concentrate on hanging on to the back of the bear and that dissipated some of his fear.

The bear still had the bottom of his sleeping bag firmly in its mouth and Tyler had a death grip on its furry rear haunches. They raced along with the other bear in hot pursuit. The bear was going up a steep incline but as hard as Tyler tried to look out, there was nothing to see. It was still deep in the night.

The bears continued up the mountain, both wanting to have the entire delicious treat. Tyler had no idea what would happen when they found the juicy boy inside the bag, but he was sure he didn't want to find out.

Chapter 3

After what must have been several hours of bouncing along up and down mountains Tyler heard the bear laboring in great huffs of breath and the other bear sounded like it was falling behind. Tyler had been working on the zipper with one hand and holding on with the other. The zipper wouldn't budge. He had brought his small pack inside with him and he careful lowered one hand inside the sleeping bag and pulled the pack into his lap. He reached in and grasped his hunting knife and using his thumb he unsnapped the leather strap that kept the knife in the sheath.

The knife was a gift from his grandfather and, with his father looking on, he had been allowed to use it and carry it when his dad took him hunting. Tyler loved the knife and between his dad and grandpa, they instructed him in how to care for and sharpen the blade.

Tyler looked out of the opening and could see it was full daylight now and the bears were slowing. He thought that soon they would both stop and either fight over the bag or join in consuming the food inside.

Tyler Hill's Decision

It was time to do something and like his mama always told him, "When it's time to do something, don't wait around thinking somebody else is going to do it for you; just get up and do it and then you don't have to worry with it anymore!"

He had both hands in the thick fur but in his right hand he had a grip on his knife as well. He brought the blade down to the zipper and drew it across the cloth webbing. The webbing gave way but not just a little. The cloth ripped open all the way to the bottom of the bag, spilling Tyler out. He just had time to grab his small pack before he was tumbling through the bushes, trying to keep the blade of the knife away from his body. As he rolled he looked out and saw the other bear that was chasing his bear look over at him but it didn't stop. Tyler guessed that peanut butter would taste better anyway or at least he hoped so.

Tyler came to a sudden stop against a medium size tree and the air whooshed out of him. He felt a stabbing pain in his side as he tried to regain his breath. It took a long time for the air to start to fill his lungs again and it frightened him because his lungs felt frozen. Finally they began to work but he was trying so hard to breathe that when the air started to return to his lungs it came in a loud whistling noise and too slow. The harder he tried to take a breath the louder the noise came from his mouth, but he needed air and kept trying to bring the sweet air into his lungs.

After a few minutes his breathing returned to normal and he lay beside the tree trying to determine how badly he was hurt. He still had a stabbing pain in his side but it was getting better. He could move his arms and legs without pain, but he decided to lie there for a while just to rest. His whole body ached from the jostling ride he took on the back of that bear. He looked at the trunk of the tree and noticed the flakes of bark that were hanging from it. The trunk was gray and blotched with darker spots. It was a hickory-nut tree and it went straight up to the sky. He looked at the other treetops around him and he saw big pine trees, water oak, live oak and red oak trees, along with red buds and dogwood trees. He noticed as he turned his head that he could look out to his right and see the tops of big trees, which seemed a little odd to him. He slowly sat up and saw he was on the side of a mountain and that was why he could look out and see the tops of the trees that were lower down the slope.

He moved his arms and legs again and found the pain in his side gone, but he still felt like he had been dragged behind a car.

He chuckled, thinking, 'It wasn't a car but a bear… a big bear!'

He saw his pack was lying beside him and he still gripped his knife in his right hand. He reached in the pack and returned the knife to its sheath and closed the flap. It was then he heard that now familiar sniffing sound. The fear jumped through his body and he tried to freeze but his head snapped around of its own accord. The two bears had returned. They both looked comical with goose feathers in their mouths and all in their fur. It looked like they had a big duck breakfast, but Tyler guessed that it was the last of his sleeping bag. The problem was— now they were looking at him and they still looked hungry.

Tyler Hill's Decision

Tyler tried his best not to look them in the eyes but he couldn't make his eyes obey. He kept glancing at the two bears and tried to remember more rules about meeting a bear in the woods.

'Was it; don't run uphill or downhill? Am I supposed to climb a tree? No, that couldn't be right because everyone knows bears can climb trees.'
The bears were moving closer to him so he slowly stood up.

Tyler was fourteen years old and tall for his age. He took after his dad and his dad was a big man. The bears stopped when he stood up but their gaze never left him and the hungry look was still there. Even with a mouthful of feathers they looked serious. One and then the other stood on their hind legs, making them much taller than Tyler, and they roared with their heads shaking from side to side and drool was flying from their mouths. Their fangs looked like they had grown to twice the size they were the night before. Tyler did what every red-blooded man would do in a situation like this. He turned and ran!

Chapter 4

Even in his fright Tyler's mind was working out a way to get out of the problem he was facing.

His dad made a game with Tyler, his brother and sister called *'What would you do if?'* He would tell them adventure stories and during the telling he would ask them what they would do in that situation. He always told them that no matter how hard or scary the problem was there was always a way out.

Since Tyler couldn't remember which way he was supposed to run— uphill or down— he took off running around the mountain. It surprised the bears so much that it took them a few seconds to realize that their breakfast had left but then they took off after it.

Tyler was running along a narrow trail of some kind and it made the going easier. It took him into thick stands of mountain laurel, bushes with tangled limbs, thick green leaves and large pink flowers. The trail was so narrow that in places he had to squeeze between the thick limbs. He could hear the bears crashing through the tangle behind him and the noise gave him more speed to get away from them. He could hear the bears struggling and it sounded like they were getting angrier as they roared out their displeasure.

Tyler was through the tangles and running full speed, with spider webs wrapping around his head and body and limbs slapping him as he ran. He didn't like the webs wrapping around his face and he looked down for an instant and saw a big black spider on his shirt and making its way up toward his face. He slapped at the spider and took his eyes off the trail. He tripped on a root and went sprawling onto his stomach. He jumped up and looked behind him and both bears were racing toward him and were only about twenty feet away.

As they rushed in for their feast Tyler stepped behind a giant red oak tree and the bears tumbled into each other trying to stop. One bear bit down on the rear end of the other one and that bear slapped the biter with his powerful paw. They turned to face each other for an instant but then remembered the reason they were there.

Tyler made his way around the trunk of the tree and on the uphill side he came to a tall, narrow opening in the trunk. It looked big enough for him to squeeze in but too small for the bears. He couldn't decide what to do until he heard the bears crashing through the brush just on the other side of the tree. Tyler squeezed into the opening and found himself in a tree cave big enough for him to stand. He looked up and could see light streaming into the cave about twenty feet above him. He quickly looked around and could see that the inside of the giant tree was not smooth but had what looked like shelves of dead wood going up the inside of the tree.

He heard a tremendous roar and jumped back away from the opening just in time as a big paw swiped at him. He had his back pressed against the side of the cave out of reach of the bear's paw. He watched with apprehension as the bear felt around inside the cave looking for him. The bear's paw came back to the entrance and hooked on the edge of the opening. With terrific strength the bear tore a hunk of the entranceway loose and pulled it out of the way. He put his paw back in and tore another large piece away and then stuck his head in and snapped his great jaws at Tyler, only a feet few away from his legs. The bear tried to bring his large paw in but there wasn't room at the entrance for his massive head and front paw. He backed out and the other big bear stuck his head in and looked directly at Tyler. Tyler could see the madness in its eyes and also the hunger.

He could smell peanut butter and dead things on its breath as it huffed and sniffed at him. Tyler guessed that the bag full of feathers wasn't enough to satisfy their hunger. The bear continued to look at him and huff, getting Tyler's scent. The look in the bear's eyes left no doubt in Tyler's mind that it meant business and it was angry at being fooled by this little animal.

The bear pulled his head out and it too used its paw to tear a piece of the entrance away. Tyler could see that it would soon be big enough for the bears to get to him. He looked up again at the light above him. As he turned around his foot hit something solid and he bent down to feel a hard piece of wood about two inches around and a foot long. He picked it up and could see a sharp point at one end. It was a piece of heartwood and felt very strong. As he looked at the wood one of the bears reached in and one of his claws snagged the bottom of Tyler's shirt. Tyler felt himself being pulled towards the entrance and he spun trying to break free. He raised the piece of wood and stabbed at the paw that had his shirt. The sharp wood went into the bear's paw and it roared in pain and snatched its paw out of the cave, breaking off the wood that had buried in its paw. It let out another roar of pain and anger and that was all Tyler needed to push him into action.

Tyler turned, reached up and grabbed a piece of wood above his head and pulled himself up. Just as his feet found purchase above the floor he looked down and saw one of the bears tear a larger piece of tree from the entrance and stick the whole front of its body in and tear out the inside of the cave right where Tyler had been standing only a few seconds before.

As the bear in its frenzy tore at the inside of the cave Tyler began to climb as quickly as he could. If he had had time to think, he would have enjoyed the climb. It was like climbing a tall bookshelf. There were handholds and footholds spaced evenly up the inside of the tree. He moved as quickly as he could, trying to get away from the roar of the bear. The inside of the tree was like a megaphone and the sound of the bear hurt his ears.

In just a few moments he reached the opening where the morning light was streaming through. He looked out at the top of a massive limb that reached far out into the air. The opening was just big enough for him to squeeze through and he was soon sitting with his back against the trunk of the tree, breathing hard from exertion and fear. As his breathing slowed and he gained control of his emotions, he looked over the edge of the great limb.

Chapter 5

Tyler could see only one bear and it was peering into the cave. It let out a roar and swiped out with its paw. Tyler felt a thump inside the tree and then the other bear backed out of the cave, turned and roared at the other. Tyler knew he had moved just in the nick of time to avoid being eaten by the bears. He moved slightly to get a better view and a large piece of bark broke loose and fell, hitting one of the bears in the head. Both bears raised their heads and looked up at Tyler looking down at them.

They began to circle the tree, glancing up from time to time looking for a way to get at their food. Tyler also looked up to see if he should climb to the top of the tree but the tree was so large; the next limb was ten feet above him. He thought he might be able to grab the loose bark and make his way up but then he remembered how easily the bark had broken off and fell on the bear. He reached out, grabbed a piece of bark and pulled. A piece about two feet long broke off in his hand. He took aim at one of the bears and threw it. The flake of bark hit the bear in the right ear and it jumped and took another bite at its partner. They fought for a moment but soon stopped and looked up at Tyler. Tyler began to think maybe throwing things at them was not a good idea because one of the bears reached up with its front paws spread wide and slammed its claws into the tree. With its hind legs it leaped up and buried it rear claws into the trunk. It then with lightning speed moved its front paws up the tree and clung to the trunk. It was climbing the tree.

Tyler looked around desperately trying to decide what to do. He knew he couldn't stay where he was. He looked out at the long limb he was sitting on and could see that it ended far out over the slope of the mountain and very high above the ground. As he stood to move out on the limb he heard a loud crash and looked down. The bear that had been trying to climb the tree was lying on its back and looked dazed. The other bear looked up at Tyler and then sat down and licked at the feathers which still clung to its fur. The bear that fell rolled over, looked around like it was trying to see if anyone had seen him fall, then gave a hard look up at Tyler and then lay down.

Tyler sat back down and waited to see if the bears would leave. He waited for over an hour and neither bear had moved from its spot below the tree. Tyler didn't know what to do but he felt safe up in the tree. He guessed that it was only around twelve o'clock and he had a long day ahead of him. He opened his pack to see what he had with him and then he noticed he wasn't wearing his boots or socks. His feet were scratched and dirty from his run through the forest. He only had a long-sleeved tee shirt and his blue jeans on, which he wore when he went to sleep, thinking it would be warmer.

There wasn't anything he could do about it now so like his dad always said, "If you can't do anything about it, then don't worry about it."

He went back to looking through his pack. He had his knife, which he attached to his belt. There were two chocolate Power Bars, a compass, small towel, toothbrush and paste, a pair of socks, and his trusty flashlight. He pulled the compass out with some relief, which turned to alarm when he saw that the face was smashed and the needle missing.

Both his grandpa and dad had made it a rule that any time they went in the woods they would always take a compass. His grandpa had told Tyler that no matter how well you know the woods you are in there will be a time when you get confused and a compass will lead you back home. Tyler looked up through the treetops trying to determine which way was north, but he couldn't tell because the sun was directly overhead. He would have to wait until late afternoon and then he would know which direction was west.

He looked down again and the two bears appeared to be asleep and in no hurry to leave. He thought about eating one of the Power Bars but decided that he wasn't that hungry yet. He had no idea how long it would take for the others to find him. He didn't know where he was or how far away the others were. He had ridden on the back of the bear for what seemed like hours, traveling up and down the mountains. He smiled at the thought of telling his family and friends about how he rode a big black bear just like a horse. He might have to leave out the part of being trapped in his sleeping bag covered in peanut butter, at least to his friends. He would have some mean words for his friend Lamar when he got back. Maybe one day it would be funny but right now it didn't feel so funny.

Tyler thought about some of the stories his grandpa and dad told him about things that had happened to them. Grandpa was a sailor or at least he had several sailboats. He and Grandma would take their three kids sailing almost every week during the summertime. They even took the boat to the ocean for summer vacation. It was not a big boat but all five of them could sleep in it.

During the day the kids would take the dingy and fly around the lake or near the boat when they went to the ocean. Grandma wasn't crazy about sailing, especially when the boat heeled over in the wind, but she enjoyed the time spent with her family. She was the fisherman of the family and always had a line out behind the sailboat. Grandpa would laugh and say he had the only bass boat with sails on Lake Lanier. It all sounded like a lot of fun to Tyler. His dad said he used to hate being cooped up with his brother, sister, mom and dad for two or three days every week, but now that he was grown, he said it was a great way to grow up.

Tyler's dad tried to do all the things he had done as a kid with his family but he was very busy at work and couldn't always get away. Tyler could see his father worrying about it sometimes and he would hear his mom talking softly to his dad, telling him it was all

Tyler Hill's Decision

right and that he was a good father. Tyler thought when he got back home he would tell his whole family how much he loved them and especially his dad.

The sun was low in the western sky and Tyler took note of where west was. He glanced down at the bears and they hadn't moved. He could hear snores coming from them from time to time but he knew they were alert. He had thrown a piece of bark out as far as he could an hour before and both bears had come to their feet and listened intently for any noise.

Tyler had listened to the sounds of the forest all day in hopes of hearing someone calling his name, but all he heard were birds chirping and singing as they went about looking for food. He remained quiet and several time gray squirrels and chipmunks had come very close to him until they realized that he wasn't part of the tree. Then they would squeal and bark for twenty minutes letting all the other animals know that there was an intruder in the forest. Tyler began to dislike the squirrels for making so much of a racket, but as he watched the forest he saw that they could be used to his advantage.

If he were quiet and still, the animals would move around him and ignore him. Once a dog or maybe a small wolf came near but Tyler knew it was coming long before he saw it. The squirrels deep in the forest would set up a racket and as the dog traveled they would signal to each other where he was. Tyler thought of it as a dog because he didn't want to think of wolves traveling in the forest where he was. Dogs weren't too bad but wolves would eat you.

He looked out at the forest and it quickly began to darken with the coming of night. The sky was still bright but the treetops cast deep shadows all around him. Tyler didn't want to stay in the forest by himself all night. He was beginning to dislike the mountains and thought if he ever got out of there he would not be back for a long time. As he watched the light fade he glanced down to see two black blobs where the bears slept. Soon it was pitch black and as he looked up he could only see a star now and again as the boughs moved in the wind.

Tyler had forced himself to stay awake all day but as the blue sky overhead took on a light pink and then bright orange his eyes drooped with fatigue. He wondered how he would be able to sleep sitting on the limb. He had found a snag inside the tree to hang his pack on, but now he worried about falling out of the tree if he went to sleep.

He tried lying face down on the limb, letting his arms hang out to his sides and found he was pretty secure like that as long as he didn't roll around while he slept. He could barely hold his eyes open and was soon fast asleep. During the long night he awoke often, feeling like he was falling but only found that the bark was digging into his face. The forest sounded much different at night. Few birds sounded. He heard the leaves rustling as animals moved near his tree and once he thought he heard a baby crying but he remembered that a wildcat made a sound like that. It was an eerie cry and sent chills through his already cold body. Once during the night he awoke to hear the huffs of the bears below and it sounded like they were moving away from the tree. Tyler hoped they were giving up on the meal that slept in the tree above them.

He awoke just before dawn to the sound of silence. Nothing seemed to be stirring in the dark. He sat up and rested his back against the trunk of the tree and tried to look around him, but all he could see were stars overhead through the branches of the tree. Tyler kept his eyes open and after a short while he realized that he could see the outline of the trees around him and, as if on cue, the forest came alive with sound. Birds began to sing and small animals scurried through the leaves that covered the floor of the forest. As he looked, the shapes of the trees began to take on more detail and color was coming from behind the mountain. The day didn't arrive like the night. It slowly spread its light through the forest and Tyler began to feel better, now that he could look around. A small herd of deer moved slowly around the mountain, nuzzling through the leaves in search of acorns and mushrooms. He peered down the trunk of the tree and the bears were gone.

Chapter 6

He felt a surge of pleasure at finally being free from the bears and he hoped they were far away by now. Tyler remained very still, like when his papa took him deer hunting. He used only his eyes to observe the forest around him. He carefully examined each bush and tree in the area, looking for signs of the two bears. He didn't know how smart bears were but he didn't give them much credit. After all, they had eaten a sleeping bag full of feathers. Only the squirrels and chipmunks scurried along the ground, busily gathering nuts and acorns, getting ready for the winter to come.

Tyler waited for what felt like two hours before he stood up and stretched, trying to ease his sore muscles and stiff back. He continued to watch and listen for another hour before he ventured down to the ground to try to find his friends. He decided not to eat anything even though he was hungry. He didn't want the smell of chocolate to bring the bears back. He figured if they liked peanut butter so much then chocolate would drive them crazy. He gathered his pack, making sure it was closed, and then made his way into the hollow of the tree. It was an easy climb down and he was soon standing at the bottom of the tree cave. Still he waited, listening for any sound of something big moving around.

He cautiously moved out of the cave and stood very still for a few minutes. He didn't want to meet the two bears again. He slowly moved away from the trunk of the tree and then stopped to consider his next move. He figured he should go east because that would lead out of the mountains. The sun had risen on the other side of the mountain and he looked up the steep slope, thinking that that would be a hard climb. He saw the trail leading around the mountain and decided it would be much easier to walk around the mountain than to climb over it. He did want to climb mountains but not this morning and not in his bare feet. He started off slowly, listening for any sounds that would alert him to danger. Even the squirrels seemed to ignore him as he moved quietly through the forest.

Now that he had time to look around, this really was a beautiful place. The trees were massive and tall and their canopy formed a roof that allowed shafts of sunlight to pierce through to the floor of the forest. He tried to name all the trees he saw but there were many he didn't recognize. He saw oak, hickory, ash, beech, small red buds and clumps of laurel with their thick, leathery, green leaves and large pink flowers.

The ground was covered in last year's leaves and small bushes. Some had tiny white flowers covering them and the bees were busy gathering the nectar to make honey. He passed through a few open glades filled with wildflowers and knee-high grass. In several places he saw where the grass had been laid flat and knew from his dad and grandpa that this was where a herd of deer had slept. He was feeling proud, and all the things they had told him were making him feel better about being all alone in the mountains.

As the morning wore on the sun warmed things up nicely. He found a small cliff face where water was running out of the rocks forming a small pool. He was very thirsty so he stopped and drank his fill. There were small fish in the pool and Tyler wondered how they got all the way up this mountain and found their way into the pool. He would ask his dad when he got back. He was really looking forward to seeing his family again. He didn't mind being alone as long as he knew his family was close by, but out here, having no idea where he was, was not his idea of good alone-time.

The drink of water made him hungry. He hadn't eaten since two nights ago so he took one of the Power Bars from his pack. He sat down next to the pool and slowly ate the chocolate bar. It was delicious. As he was finishing the bar he heard the now familiar sniffing.

It came from down the mountain and it sounded like it was close. He quickly looked around but saw nowhere to hide. He ran as quietly as he could along the path. He knew if he took off through the forest he would make a racket in the dry leaves. Now the squirrels were chattering away telling everyone where he was. This spurred him on even faster. He ran for what must have been a halfmile and stopped to catch

Tyler Hill's Decision

his breath. As his breathing slowed he listened intently for the sound he had heard earlier. He picked up a smooth, round rock just to have something to throw if he needed to. He was leaning against the trunk of a very large oak tree, listening. He waited twenty minutes and heard nothing that sounded dangerous. He decided to keep moving around the mountain. He moved to his left, making his way around the trunk of the tree and came face-to-tail with the two bears!

Tyler didn't stop to think. He turned and moved quickly back around the trunk of the giant tree. As he moved he threw the stone down the mountainside. It made a racket as it rolled down the steep slope and the bears heard it and took off down the mountain after it. Tyler didn't wait to see what happened next. He moved off quietly down the trail, trying to put as much distance between him and the bears as he could. He had been walking fast for fifteen minutes when he heard leaves rustling down the slope and behind him. He glanced over his shoulder and saw the bears at the same time they saw him. They both let out a roar of anger and began to run up the slope. Tyler took off down the trail as fast as he could. The bears were moving quickly, crashing through the brush.

Tyler thought as he ran, 'I guess bears go uphill just as fast as they go downhill.'

He was still well ahead of the bears but he could hear them getting closer as they grunted with effort with each stride they took. He knew they could run for a long time when food was involved and he didn't think he could keep ahead of them for much longer. He was getting extremely tired. He rounded a curve on the trail and saw a smaller trail off to his right heading downhill at an angle. It ran straight into a clump of laurel bushes but there was a small tunnel under the outstretched limbs. He took the right fork and ran for the laurel. He dropped to his hands and knees and scrambled through the thicket. As he passed to the other side and stood he heard a tremendous roar and looked back to see both bears crashing into the thicket. They looked angry and hungry all at the same time. They were ripping the limbs from the Laurel bushes and making their way towards Tyler. He turned and sprinted away down the path.

Tyler could hear them come out of the thicket, huffing as they picked up speed pursuing him. He looked around desperately trying to find somewhere to go to get away from them. Ahead he saw another fork in the small trail. One branch started to angle uphill and the other turned and went straight downhill and it led to another thicket of some kind of thick bushes. Tyler was tired and didn't know how much longer he could keep going before the bears caught up with him. He didn't think he could run uphill for very long so he turned down the trail and ran for the bushes.

Chapter 7

He scrambled under the tightly packed limbs on his hands and knees. As he exited the thicket he glanced back over his shoulder and saw both bears snarling and running at full speed down the hill. Tyler ran as fast as he could and after about fifty yards he saw a light ahead of him through a thicket of thin blueberry bushes. He ran full speed into the bushes and the limbs grabbed at his shirt and pants but he didn't even notice. He burst out of the bushes at full speed and came out onto a large flat rock. Ten feet in front of him there was nothing, only open sky and a background of green far away. He didn't have time to react but did see a thin red bud tree hanging out in the air just to his left. He tried to stop but his bare feet skidded and he went over the edge of the cliff with his hands spread like he might have to learn to fly—quickly!

His left hand hit the spindly red bud tree and it closed around the top of the trunk with an iron grip. His momentum was stopped and as he swung to his left he brought his right hand around and grasped the trunk. The tree was so thin that it bent under his weight and lowered him down below the top of the rock ledge and swung him further to the left. Tyler could hear the bears huffing and crashing.

They burst through the berry bushes at top speed and were so blinded by their anger that they never slowed as they plunged off the top of the flat rock. They were halfway down before they realized what had happened and each let out a roar. The roars were cut off sharply as they hit the rocks one hundred feet below.

Tyler was busy trying to hold on to the tree but he had time to look out and watch both bears as they seemed to float out into the empty air. He only got a quick look as they passed by and then he turned his attention to saving himself. The red bud lowered him to the rock face. It was cracked and broken with small openings. He reached out and grabbed for a handhold and found that the rocks were firmly anchored in the face of the cliff. He soon had a foothold as well and he released his grip on the thin tree. As he released it he took time to admire the tiny red flowers that covered its limbs. They had a slight fragrance as the limbs shook and waved in the air now that it was free from Tyler's grip. He turned his attention to the cliff and found numerous hand and footholds to make the climb back to the top, only ten feet above his head.

He reached the top and flopped over onto the flat rock. He lay there for a long time letting his heart slow down and his breathing return to normal. Now that he had some time to think about what just happened, he began to shake all over. He had read in some adventure books about how adrenaline rushed through your body and gave you incredible strength but afterwards it left you shaking as it coursed through your body. He wasn't really afraid so he now understood what the stories were talking about. He slowly sat up and let his legs dangle over the drop-off. Now that he had time to look around he looked down into a beautiful valley. It was about a half mile wide and on the other side was a stream or small river that ran along the valley floor. He remembered his grandpa telling him that if he was ever lost and he could find a stream that he should follow it downstream because someone always lives near running water.

As he admired the view he suddenly thought about the two bears. He leaned over the cliff and looked down but could only see the tops of trees far below, with leaves still floating around from the earlier disturbance. He heard no sounds of bears and he didn't know how to feel about what had happened.

He was glad the bears were gone but he thought it might be his fault that they were dead or injured. He gave it a lot of thought as he rested and couldn't quite decide how to feel. Like his dad said about not being able to do anything about it— he put his thoughts in the back of his mind and started thinking about something he could do something about.

He needed to find his friends or really anybody to help him get out of the mountains. He needed to call his parents and let them know he was all right and he needed to find more water. He looked at his feet and saw that they were cut and bleeding but they didn't hurt too much.

He wanted to go down to the valley but he wasn't about to climb down the cliff. It was way too far to the bottom and he didn't want to meet up with the bears again, dead or alive. He looked down at the stream and could see the water flowing west. He was pretty sure he needed to go east but remembering what his grandpa had told him, he decided to move towards the west in the direction he had come from. He would slowly work his way down the slope of the mountain and hoped he would make it down to the valley before dark. It was sometime after noon and he didn't look forward to sleeping in the mountains alone again that night.

Chapter 8

He took his time, watching where he put his feet, trying not to make a lot of noise and not wanting to step on anything sharp. He found a few small trails and followed them for a while, until they turned uphill. He had made up his mind to make for the valley below and he would stick to the plan. He knew if nothing else it would be easier to travel on flat ground and being near the stream he wouldn't have to worry about his thirst.

He reached the valley floor as the sun passed behind the mountains to the west. It was still daylight and the trees were spaced well apart, giving him light to see by. He had to find a place to stay that night and he looked around desperately hoping to see smoke or evidence that there were people around.

He could see no sign of people and he started to feel like he was the last person on earth. The feeling gripped his heart and he could feel the tears start to well up.

He rubbed his eyes, took a deep breath and said, "Don't go acting like a baby! You've been camping plenty of times and it's about time to be on your own for a day or two."

He took another deep breath and felt better as he looked around. He moved through open glades of grass and flowers and soon heard the sound of running water. As he came closer to the stream the brush grew thicker but he found a path through to the stream. He came out at a clear pool with smooth rocks covering the bottom. He kneeled down and took a long drink and the icy water made him feel much better. He looked around and in the sand beside the pool where the trail crossed it he noticed tracks.

He moved over to look at them and there were deer prints and some small animal prints. What got his attention was what looked like several big dog prints. He hoped that was a good sign that people were somewhere around because he knew dogs didn't live off by themselves unless they were wild.

He crossed the stream and moved away from it, looking for a place to stay for the night. He saw a thick bramble of thorny bushes and he moved close. The light was dimming with the coming of night and as he bent down he could see a narrow low trail leading into the bramble. He thought the long thorns might give him some protection so he got down on his hands and knees and started into the bushes. He quickly had to lie on his belly and crawl because the thorns were catching in his shirt and sticking into his back. He crawled for perhaps ten feet and came to an opening. He sat up and looked around and found evidence of a small fire that had only a few charred sticks left in a cleared area. He made his decision to stay there for

Tyler Hill's Decision

the night and looked to find a place to lie down. As he moved to the edge of the small cleared area in the dim light he noticed big dark berries hanging from the bushes. He reached out and pulled one off the branch and smelled it. It was a blackberry! He took a small bite and the dark juicy flowed into his mouth and made him smile. He loved blackberry cobbler that his mom made and even the Thai food Grandma made using blackberries his grandpa and Tyler picked for her.

It was now too dark to see so he took out his flashlight and quickly gathered two handfuls of berries and then settled down for his small meal. The sweetness of the berries put him in a better mood and he began to relax. He had had a tough day and even though his feet were hurting, he was soon asleep.

His dreams were of his brother, Nick, and sister, Kasia, looking all through the house for him. They were calling his name and Kasia was crying with worry. Then he was back on the flat rock at the top of the cliff, standing with his back to the drop-off and the two bears were in front of him with their long fangs gleaming. He took a step back from their fierce snarls and he fell off the cliff. He was flying through the air on his way to the bottom.

He awoke with a start and tried to catch his breath. It was pitch black and he couldn't see anything. His breathing began to slow as he realized it had been a dream. He lay back down and listened to the night. He could hear the night creatures scurrying around and his eyes slowly closed and he was back asleep in a moment. He awoke every few minutes all night long and he would listen to the night for danger.

It was a long night for him and as it began to grow light in the east he fell into an exhausted sleep.

Tyler awoke a few hours later and felt refreshed but as he sat up and looked around he could see that the sun was high in the east. He had slept through most of the morning. He moved through the bramble on his belly and walked to the stream. He was angry that he had wasted so much time. He should have been several miles down the valley searching for anyone who could help him or tell him where he was. After a long, cool drink of water he reached in his bag for his last Power Bar but then remembered the blackberries. He should save his food for as long as he could in case he had to spend another night in the forest. He went back to the bushes and used the bottom of his shirt to hold the berries he picked. As he walked along near the stream he enjoyed the succulent fruit. When he had finished off the last of the berries he looked at the bottom of his shirt and saw that it was stained purple.

He thought, 'Mom will never get this stain out. I hope she won't be mad.'

The more he thought about it, the more he didn't care. He just wanted to see his mom again and tell her he loved her. He would tell every one of his family that. It had been a long time since he had said those words and he knew it hurt his dad because he told Tyler every day how much he loved him.

Tyler had been upset for a long time and no one except his dad, Uncle Jason and Aunt Ginda seemed to understand what he was going through. The guys at school and even a few of his friends had started to tease him at the beginning of the school year. They wanted to know what he was, and he always answered that he was black, Thai, white and maybe some Indian. The answer didn't sit well with him but he didn't know what else to say. It was true; he was all those things and he felt like if he could be just one it would be so much easier for him. Most of the girls never asked him stupid questions like that. A few had said they liked him but he didn't show them much attention. His dad always said the boys were just jealous of him because he was such a handsome young man. Tyler knew that his dad was just saying that to make him feel better and it really didn't count. He shook off his train of thought and looked around.

He had been walking downstream and the bushes were getting thicker. He turned right and headed toward the center of the valley. Ten yards away from the stream the ground opened up and the walking was much easier. He decided to follow the stream but not stay so close until he needed a drink or to take a break. The floor of the valley looked like it might have been a farm a long time ago. It was flat and had only a few large old trees growing. In a few places there were groves of oaks and in others there were short gnarled trees with small fruit growing on them. He stopped to examine a few and the fruit looked like tiny apples but they were too young to eat. He hoped he wouldn't be around long enough to eat them when they were ripe. There were open glades that looked like old fields. The wildflowers filled them with every color he could think of. In some places stands of tall, straight pines grew in rows like someone had planted them, years before.

His mind began to wander and he thought about what it must have been like to live way out here in the mountains back when the first settlers came. It must have been hard work without tractors and trucks. They must have been afraid of wild Indians that roamed the mountains just looking for someone to kill and steal their food and horses. When he thought of that he stopped and felt a little ashamed because he knew he had a little Cherokee Indian blood in him.

His grandpa mentioned it often and was proud of the fact that he was part Indian. He told Tyler that his great-grandmother had been a full-blooded Cherokee and while he was growing up he told everyone about that. Tyler never really understood why he was so proud of being an Indian. He certainly didn't look like one, although Tyler had never actually seen one face to face. He had only seen pictures of them in his history book and a few of the adventure stories he had read. Everything he had read made it seem like all they did was make war on white people and each other.

It was past noon and the heat of the day was starting to make him sweat. He moved in close to the stream and found a small pool of cool, clear water. He took a long drink and then let his feet dangle in the flowing stream. As he looked in the water he saw movement. He looked closer and saw a number of fish about six or seven inches long swimming in the current. They looked beautiful and delicious. He thought of a story his dad had told him. He said you could catch fish with your bare hands if you had enough patience.

"Now, what was it I am supposed to do?"

He moved slowly across the stream and lay down on a rock overhang and went still.

Slowly the fish came back out of the hiding place and were soon just hanging in the water, moving their tails once in a while. He slowly lowered his hands into the water and made a U shape with his fingers and thumb. Several of the fish came to investigate and even moved into the shape of his hand. He slowly closed his fingers but they would just swim out from his touch. He lowered his hands so that his palms were facing up. He lay there for over five minutes while the fish remained motionless in the current and then two fish came to his hands and seem to settle in. With a quick movement he lifted both hands and flung the fish out onto the bank. He jumped up and across the small stream and grabbed them before they could flip back into the water.

Tyler was so happy at his accomplishment that he forgot about being in the mountains alone for a few minutes. He searched his pack and found the cheap lighter in an inside pocket. He normally wasn't allowed to carry a lighter around but his grandpa had whispered that he should always take one with him when he went into the woods. He said it was much easier to build a small fire with a lighter than by rubbing two sticks together. Tyler laughed at the thought of making a fire with sticks but he wondered what the old mountain men had used.

He cut some thin green limbs from a nearby bush and ran one through the gills of the fish to keep them from flopping away. He went about gathering dead limbs and twigs, cleared out an area under a large tree at the edge of one of the clearings and started a small fire. He quickly cleaned the fish but left the heads on so he had some way to secure them to the thin limbs. Leaving the heads on didn't bother him like it might some of his friends. His grandma cooked fish, often leaving the heads on. He guessed that's the way it was done in Thailand. She even showed him that some of the best meat was on the cheeks of the fish.

His fire was small but nice and hot as he pushed the sticks into the ground and moved the fish over the fire. He wasn't sure how long it would take to cook a fish but he did know that it wouldn't be long. The few times his mom had let him cook some of the fish they had caught he had burnt them, until his mom showed him how to check the meat with a fork to see if it was flaky.

He sat with his back to the large oak tree and enjoyed his meal. They needed some salt but for catching them with nothing but his hands they were good. Tyler thought more about how the people who first came to mountains survived and about the Indians that were here before them. It must have been a hard life but to live off the land must have been rewarding also. He finished his meal, poured water from the stream on the fire and scattered the limbs to make sure it was out, and then he continued moving further into the valley, hoping to find someone soon.

Tyler Hill's Decision

While he walked he heard noises that sounded like footsteps a few times but when he looked carefully around he saw no one. He didn't call out but he did listen for voices of people looking for him. He knew by now that there would be a lot of people searching. He hoped his family wasn't worried. He really missed his older brother and sister. He looked all around as he walked and saw that this was a beautiful place. The valley was a halfmile wide and the mountains rose up steeply on both sides. The mountains were covered in different shades of green and it reminded him of some of the pictures he had seen of Scotland. The valley was covered in wildflowers and stands of trees almost like a park or large garden and he was the only one there to see it.

As he rested under a beechnut tree a herd of deer came out of the trees and slowly made their way across a field. They were very cautious and every few steps they would stop and look around for danger. They were Whitetail deer but they kept their flags hidden. Tyler had seen them in the woods near his house and when they were frightened they would lift their tails, which were pure white on the bottom, and wave them like a flag as they bound away. He watched them for ten minutes but he knew he had to keep moving in hopes of finding his way out or finding someone else.

It was late in the afternoon and the sun was just touching the tops of a western mountain. Tyler started looking for another clump of bushes to sleep in. He crossed the creek and moved to the edge of the valley searching for just the right place. Something caught his eye down in the valley and he stopped to see what it was.

There was a tiny spark of light far down the valley. A house! That had to be a light from a house and that meant people! He started moving quickly as the light of day turned the sky to a brilliant orange and painted the clouds that had moved in over the valley. Within a few minutes it was dark and Tyler looked up in the sky and saw more stars than he had ever seen before. Even though he was in a hurry to find the house that was ahead of him, he stopped and looked at the sky. It was painted with sparkling lights so thick they almost seemed to touch one another. He wanted to remember this so he could tell his dad about it.

The light ahead was like a beacon. Tyler had read about lighthouses that warned sailors about dangerous waters but some had shown them the way home and were welcome sights to the sailors at sea. He hoped this one would be a welcoming beacon but as he got closer he thought about being cautious and not rushing into the light. The light would blink off and on every once in a while and he didn't understand why but he kept moving toward it. He tried his best not to make any noise but he stepped on a twig or dead limb a few times and they made loud cracks as they broke. He slowed down and tried to move softly. He wasn't sure why but he wanted to see whoever was out there.

Tyler moved slowly towards the light and he saw it was not a light from a house but a campfire of some kind. There was no one around but he could smell meat cooking and there was a pot beside the fire that steam rose from with a delicious aroma. His mouth began to water at the thought of hot food but he kept his mind on sneaking up to see who was there. He stopped at the edge of the firelight and looked all around. He couldn't see anyone. There was a pack and some kind of sleeping bag rolled up near the trunk of a tree, small pine limbs laid out like a bed but no one around. Tyler thought maybe whoever it was had gone for a walk or to wash up at the nearby stream. He decided that while they were gone he would go into the camp and take a quick look around and try to determine who was there. He hoped it was a big group of people but he could see only one pack.

He thought about drawing his knife but he didn't want to frighten whoever was there. He moved into the light of the fire and walked over to the pack and sleeping bag. He could see footprints but they looked soft and rounded on the edges, not like a boot would make. The smell of the food turned his head toward the fire and he moved closer to the pot. There was a short stick beside the pot and he used it to lift the pot lid and looked in. As he raised the lid the aroma wafted from the pot and Tyler's mouth watered with anticipation. He was extremely hungry but it wasn't his food so he lowered the lid over the vegetables and meat that simmered beside the fire. He turned around and looked into the eyes of a big dog.

Chapter 9

The dog was staring at him with a deadly glare and suddenly a low rumble started deep in its throat and grew louder as it moved to the front of its mouth. It had its lips pulled back and large, sharp teeth glistened as the growl grew louder.

Tyler put his hands out to his side and started to ease backwards, away from the big dog. He knew it was a dog because it had short hair and long, floppy ears and had at least three different colors. It was mostly black but had grayish-blue patches of fur on its back and under its neck. There was also a tan circle of fur near its long, black tail. Even so, it looked like it could and would eat him if he made any wrong moves.

Tyler said, "Nice doggy. I was only looking. I wasn't going to take anything. Nice doggy."

From behind Tyler a voice said, "His name is Two Paws and he doesn't like to be called doggy."

Tyler screamed and jumped forward but the big dog's growl grew even louder. He started to turn to the right to run.

Tyler Hill's Decision

The voice said, "Don't run! Two Paws will think you are doing something wrong and he might attack."

Tyler froze, not knowing what to do but he didn't want the dog to attack him!

The voice did not sound angry or even mean as it said, "Turn around, young man, so that I can see who it is that comes to my camp without announcing himself."

Tyler, still with his hands out to his side, slowly turned toward the voice. The voice belonged to an older man, not much taller than Tyler. He had dark skin and long, shiny black hair that was braided and hanging over his left shoulder. He had a strong, thin nose and black eyebrows. The man had sparkling, dark eyes that seemed to be laughing but his mouth showed no hint of a smile.

Tyler said, "I'm sorry... I wasn't going to steal anything. I'm lost and need help to find my way out of the mountains."

The man asked, "Why would you want to leave these beautiful mountains? Please, put your hands down, son. I can see you mean me and my dog no harm."

Tyler lowered his arms and looked into the man's eyes. A feeling of calm came over him and tears began to glisten in his eyes at the relief of seeing another human after two days alone in the mountains.

He said in a husky voice, "I... want to get back to my family and friends. We were camping and I was attacked by two bears and they carried me off but I managed to escape."

The man's eyes widened in surprise as he spoke, "Two bears attacked you and you got away? This is a story I must hear but first let's sit down and have something to eat."

Tyler said, "My name is Tyler Hill and I am really glad to meet you, sir. I'm glad to meet just about anyone right now!"

The man gave him an odd look but then smiled and said, "My name is Walter Huie. Now, sit down and let's eat."

Walter went to his pack and brought out two bowls and spoons and a large chunk of bread. He moved to the pot and stirred the delicious thick broth inside. He spooned out a full bowl and put it on a rock beside him and then filled the other bowl.

He handed one to Tyler and Tyler started to take a big mouthful when Walter said, "Let's ask that this food be blessed before we start."

Tyler lowered his spoon into the bowl and shyly said, "I'm sorry. We always pray before we eat at home. It's just that I'm really hungry and this smells so good."

"You don't have to apologize. Just enjoy the food."

Tyler ate the entire bowl of stew and bread and for the first time in several days he felt the pleasantness of a full belly.

With his hunger sated he looked around the small camp and noticed a long bow leaning against a tree and a quiver of arrows hanging from a low limb. There was no tent but a ground cover was spread out close by. The pack Walter would carry was large and appeared to be full of items. Other than that there was little else. He looked again at Walter and wondered about his long hair that reached down almost to the small of his back. It had a colorful strip of leather tying it behind the neck. The color looked like some kind of beadwork with tiny designs in it. Walter's skin was dark but in the firelight it had a reddish tint to it. He had a strong brow and high cheekbones. There was something that Tyler recognized about him but couldn't place what it was. Suddenly an image came to his mind of an Indian with an eagle feather headdress with piercing eyes looking out across the mountains.

"Excuse me, Mr. Huie, but are you an Indian?"

Walter turned his gaze on Tyler and suddenly Tyler wished he hadn't asked that question because the fierce look that was on Walter's face bored into him and made him want to run.

Walter looked at him for a moment longer and then his expression eased and he said, "I am of the Cherokee nation and of the eastern tribe. Indian is a name you white men gave to us but today it doesn't have the same connotations as it did in the past so it doesn't upset me to be called an Indian."

"I'm... I'm sorry. I didn't mean to be rude. That's what everyone I know calls Native Americans. Even my grandpa uses that word. I'm sorry, Mr. Huie!"

Walter let a slow smile cross his face and he said, "Young Mr. Hill, you don't have to keep apologizing to me and I would like you to call me Walter. It makes me feel old to be called Mr. Huie. Is your grandfather the one with Cherokee blood in him?"

Tyler looked at him in surprise. He never really knew if he should believe his grandpa when he said he was part Indian... Cherokee. His dad said he didn't know for sure but his papa never told a story that wasn't true without telling him afterwards that it wasn't true so he believed him.

Tyler asked, "Mr. Huie... I mean Walter, how do you know my grandpa has Cherokee blood in him? And please call me Tyler."

"Well, Tyler, I can see a little of our people in you and I wondered if you knew that you too are part Cherokee."

Tyler hadn't really thought about being part Indian but it made sense that if his grandpa was part Indian... Cherokee, then he would be also.

He thought, 'I have to start saying Cherokee instead of Indian.' He said, "You will make my grandpa happy to hear you say that because when he talks about that he tells me he is proud. He told me once he was more proud of his Cherokee blood than all the other blood inside him."

Walter smiled and said, "That's enough talk for tonight. You need to rest after I take a look at your feet."

Tyler looked down at his feet and could see the dried blood and cuts and scratches on them.

He said, "That's okay. It really doesn't hurt."

Walter stood and went to a tree near his ground cover and took down a leather bucket and brought it over to Tyler. He then went to his pack and took out a small pouch and returned.

Tyler Hill's Decision

He kneeled down in front of Tyler, lifted one foot and then the other, taking a good look at them and said, "They might not hurt now but in a few days your feet will be infected so sit still and let me tend to them."

He rested Tyler's left foot on top of his knee and poured a little water over it and then carefully began to clean his foot. This was a little uncomfortable to Tyler. He wasn't used to people other than his family touching him but he could see the concern in Walter's eyes. After Walter applied an ointment to his foot, he pulled a small log over and sat the heel of Tyler's foot down on it. Walter then cleaned and applied the ointment to his right foot and sat it on the log. Walter stood and went to his pack and took out another ground cloth and extra blanket and laid them out about ten feet away from his own bedding. He stood, walked over to Tyler and bent down and lifted him up in his arms as if Tyler were a small child. He didn't show any strain on his face and Tyler could tell he was a very strong man.

Walter carried him to the ground cover and sat him down saying, "Your feet need the air to help heal them. Try not to stand and get them dirty until the morning. Two Paws will watch the camp tonight and you don't have to worry about any bears coming in during the night."

Tyler looked over and at the edge of the light he could see the big dog sleeping but his ears twitched at the sound of his name.

Walter went to his bed and was soon breathing easy with sleep. Tyler laid his head back and pulled the blanket up around his neck. It felt good. He closed his eyes for only a moment and was asleep a few seconds later.

Tyler awoke to the smell of coffee and meat frying and he was instantly hungry again. He sat up and could tell it was early. The sun hadn't risen over the tops of the mountain yet and the valley was still in the night shadows but the brightness was growing steadily as he looked out at the wildflowers in a nearby glade. He looked down at his feet, wiggled his toes and felt no pain at all. He pulled one foot up and could see the cuts were sealed and there was only a little redness around the cuts. He stood and walked over to the fire. There was still a chill in the air and the warmth of the fire felt good. He asked Walter if he could help but Walter told him to relax.

They ate a breakfast of flatbread and thin-sliced meat that had an unfamiliar taste.

"What kind of meat is this, Walter?"

Walter replied, "Bear meat."

Tyler's head snapped up and he looked at Walter.

Walter smiled and said, "Yes, that's your bear we're eating. I found them not long after they tried to fly. There was only a little meat that wasn't bruised so bad it was worth taking."

Tyler thought about this for a while and finally asked, "How long have you known I was out here?"

Walter said in a matter-of-fact tone, "I crossed your sign two days ago and followed your trail. I saw where you had caught and ate the two fish and I thought you might be someone who wanted to be alone. You seemed to be taking care of yourself,

~ 49 ~

Tyler Hill's Decision

except for the fact that you were barefoot, so I followed yesterday for a few hours. I moved ahead of you and set up camp where you could find me if you wanted to and here you are. Now I would like to hear the story of the two bears and how they tried to fly." He was smiling at his own humor and settled back to listen to Tyler.

Tyler began from when he woke up and heard the bears sniffing about. From time to time Walter would smile and once he even laughed so hard he had to hold up his hand for Tyler to stop his tale for a moment. As Tyler finished he could see the mirth in Walter's eyes.

Walter said, "That's one of the best stories I've ever heard. I will have to repeat it many times at the next meeting of the tribe. I have never heard of anyone riding on the back of a black bear!"

Tyler smiled and said, "It wasn't my idea. It just kind of happened. I really didn't have time to think about anything until I was sitting up in that tree with the two bears sleeping below me."

They both had a good laugh as they cleaned up around the camp.

As Walter packed up his gear he brought out a pair of calf-high moccasins and told Tyler to try them on. Tyler took them and felt the soft leather and admired the beautiful beadwork and leather fringe that hung from the tops.

He said, "These are too pretty to wear! I wouldn't want to get them dirty."

Walter said, "They are just boots and they were made for wearing. You won't get too far walking barefoot. They aren't too difficult to make and if you like, I will show you how."

Tyler excitedly sat down and pulled the moccasins on and tied the tops tight. They felt like nothing he had ever worn before. The soles were soft and thick and he could feel the ground as he walked around the camp.

He smiled and said, "Thank you, sir! They feel great."

Walter laughed and said, "That's the Cherokee in you. We love good moccasins."

Walter lifted his large pack, bow and quiver and started off with Two Paws leading the way.

Tyler asked, "Are you taking me to the people looking for me?"

Walter replied, "I don't know where you were, and if you rode on the back of a hungry bear for several hours, then you are many miles from where you started."

Tyler asked, "Then where are we going?"

"I have an important meeting to go to deep in the mountains. You will come with me and after the gathering is over I will take you home."

This alarmed Tyler. He was enjoying Walter's company but he wanted to see his parents again very soon. He didn't want them to worry about him and it scared him some to think he might not see them for a while. He followed along behind Walter, thinking about his dilemma. He could see Walter was a good man and meant him no harm and it would be great to spend some time in the mountains and maybe learn

Tyler Hill's Decision

something about the Cherokee people, but he needed to let his parents know he was okay.

As they walked along Walter spoke quietly about the things around them. He named the trees, birds and animals they saw. He asked Tyler a few questions to see if he was listening and could see he was worried so when they stopped for a break he asked Tyler what he was thinking about. Tyler explained that he was worried about his family and the others probably searching for him. He didn't want to be the cause of trouble, but even more, he missed his family and knew they would be very upset and worried about him.

Walter looked up at the sky and then looked towards the top of the mountain to the south and said, "We can't make it to the top before nightfall and it gets plenty cold up there at night. We will wait until morning and then go up the mountain to let everyone know you are all right."

Tyler looked up at the tall mountain and knew Walter was telling the truth. He wasn't sure how he would let everyone know but he felt a trust in this man to do just what he said he would do. He nodded and smiled.

Walter said, "Now that you trust me, Tyler, I want you to listen to the things I tell you. I don't often get a chance to share my knowledge with young men of the tribe and it pleases me to impart some of my knowledge to you. The only thing I ask is that you listen and learn. Will you do that?"

"Yes, sir. I would like that very much. I will have some great stories to tell my dad and grandpa."

Walter laughed and said, "You already have one of the best stories I have heard in a long time!"

As they continued along the floor of the valley Tyler began to listen with much more interest. He was amazed at all the things Walter knew about the forest and the animals that lived in it. He asked many questions and Walter took his time to explain it until Tyler understood. Walter also asked questions, testing Tyler's knowledge of the natural world. They stopped an hour or so before dark and set up the camp. Tyler watched Two Paws make a large circle around the camp, checking everything, and then came in, found a shady spot and went to sleep.

Walter had a cotton bag full of strips of dried meat and another with potatoes, onions and a few other vegetables. He handed Tyler a hand line and told him to go down to the stream and catch some fish.

Tyler laughed and said he could catch them with his hands, but Walter smiled and said, "It is much quicker with a hook and line."

As Tyler walked off towards the stream Two Paws jumped up and followed him.

Tyler soon returned with a nice string of fish that he held up for Walter to see.

He said, "I gave one to Two Paws for sitting with me."

Walter laughed and said, "Now you have a friend for life. He walked with you because of duty but now he likes you."

As they settled in around the small fire Walter asked Tyler if he had any questions. Tyler had been wondering about Indians all day but didn't want to sound rude so he had kept them to himself. Walter had rolled a log close to the fire and now he leaned his back against it relaxing. He took a small pouch from his vest pocket and put a little of the contents into his mouth. He told Tyler that it was chewing tobacco and it helped him relax. He sat waiting for the questions he knew Tyler wanted to ask.

Tyler told Walter he had a few questions but didn't want to offend him.

Walter laughed and said, "Ask me anything you like and I will answer as best I can, and if you say something wrong, I will correct you. I will not be offended."

Tyler finally started.

"What's it like being an Indian? Have you always lived like this?"

Walter said, "Remember, I am Cherokee. People who you call Indians are not all the same. Some live in the lowlands or out in the west on the plains and dry lands. There are many nations with different beliefs and living styles. In the past some were warlike and others tried to live in peace. The nations have a few things in common, such as a better understanding and a respect of the natural things. A long time ago the Cherokee lived close to the ocean but we slowly made our way to these mountains and lived here for many years, until the whites forced many of my people to leave our lands and move to the Indian Nations, what is now Oklahoma. Some of our tribe lived in Texas but when the whites moved into Texas they met the Apache and then the Comanche, who were warlike people. The Texans forced almost all of the different tribes out of Texas even though many were peaceful. When the Cherokee were forced to go to this new Indian Nations many died on the long march. We call it The Trail of Tears. Some stayed here, hiding far back in the mountains, and some had moved in with the whites, learning their ways, but they were always thought of as lesser people than the whites. The Cherokee people are a handsome people and many white men took Cherokee women as wives. Now there are many of our people that have the blood of others."

Tyler then asked, "The others, like my grandpa, who are only part Cherokee, what do you think of them?"

Walter smiled and said, "Remember, Tyler, you too are of the nation. We are like any other people. There are some who still hold bad feelings against the whites but most have accepted history and learned to live in the present and accept any of our blood as one of our tribe. I am one of those. I believe that if you have Cherokee in you and you respect the land and live a life that is caring and conscious of the world around you then I will call you brother. I can see many different people in you, Tyler, and I have seen how you respect the land. This is not all because of your Cherokee heritage but it is there. You have a number of nations to look upon for guidance."

Tyler thought about this and, even though he felt a little shy he wanted to ask this man whom he had learned to respect in just a few days several more questions. He thought that Walter would answer him truthfully.

Tyler Hill's Decision

He took a breath and said, "That is something I can't get straight in my mind. I do come from many different kinds of people and I don't know which one to choose when someone asks where I come from."

Walter looked at Tyler with kind eyes and said, "Who told you that you must choose?"

"Well, no one actually, but it seems to me that I must, just to answer the questions of people around me."

"What does your family say about this?"

"I haven't asked them because I know they will say things to make me feel good, but my dad and grandpa both tell me to be proud of all my heritages. My dad said he went through the same thing and so did his brother and sister but it had taken a long time to just learn to accept all of who he was."

Walter said, "I don't have an answer to the question you haven't asked, but I will say it is like your father said and you must be the one who chooses to listen to those around you or listen to yourself. You are Cherokee and would be accepted by us, but I see white, black and Asian also. All of these people have histories that you can draw upon to build your character and in the end it is all about you. If you learn to look within yourself and become a man who will make your family proud, then the answer lies there. It is your decision and those who love you can advise you but they can only lead you to the trail and then you must decide."

Walter could see the worry and indecision in Tyler's eyes and he said, "I am going to a meeting of my people and if you would like to come with me, I would be proud to introduce you to your brothers and sisters of the Cherokee nation. We will go to the top of the mountain tomorrow and you can decide then. Now, Bear Killer, it is time to sleep. Your friend Two Paws will watch the camp tonight so sleep in peace."

Tyler's eyes were wide with surprise at the name Walter called him but it also flooded him with a feeling of belonging.

He asked in a voice husky with emotions, "Do you have another name, Walter?"

As Walter stood he looked down on Tyler and a fierce blaze came to his eyes as he said, "I am called Light Foot by my people," and then he moved to his ground cover and lay down. Before Tyler could get to his bedding he could see the even breathing of Walter and knew he was already asleep.

Chapter 10

Before the light of day Walter woke Tyler and told him they had a long walk to reach the top of the mountain and then back down before nightfall. They ate a quick breakfast and started off, leaving much of the gear behind in the camp. Walter carried his bow and a small pack. He gave Tyler two canteens to carry. Walter took a trail that angled upwards on the steep slope. He asked Tyler if he had ever been sailing and Tyler said he had been a number of times with his family. Walter went on to explain that climbing a steep slope like this was similar to sailing into the wind. You had to tack up the mountain rather than trying to charge straight up. He would follow a trail for a distance and then turn ninety degrees and make his way up until he found another trail. Walter switched back and forth all the way up. Tyler asked him who made all the trails through the forest and he explained it was the animals mostly. He said they too took the easiest way up the mountain. Several hundred feet from the top the trails ended and Walter started a steeper climb. They had stopped to rest a few times but Tyler's legs were beginning to burn with fatigue.

On the climb up Tyler's mind was busy thinking about what Walter had said the night before. It was up to him to decide what kind of man he would become. He would not let his friends decide for him.

When they finally reached the top Tyler had expected to stand on a peak that came to a point and was a little disappointed that the crest of the mountain was convoluted and it was difficult to see where the highest point was. Walter led him through some thick brush and came out on a large, bare rock that overlooked the mountains and valleys for as far as the eye could see. There was a blue haze in the distance, almost like smoke from a fire, and Walter explained that this is why these mountains were called the Smoky Mountains. It was not smoke but moisture from the air as currents climbed over the mountains. Walter told Tyler to stay there and enjoy the view while he went to check something. He said he would be back in a short while.

Tyler looked out over the land at the top of the world and felt a peace he hadn't felt for a long time. There was no sign of people anywhere and it was like Walter and he were alone in a vast wilderness. He liked the idea of not having to answer all the questions of others and the only noise was of birds singing and the whisper of the wind. It relaxed his eyes to look over the expanse of this giant mountain range. He leaned back against a boulder and drifted off to sleep.

###

Tyler Hill's Decision

He was dressed in buckskin and he looked like the others around him. He had long hair tied with a beaded band around his head and he carried a bow in his left hand.

One of the young men said, "We must drive these people from our land or they will soon force us out."

Another said, "These people have done nothing to us. They have lived here for more than a year and have been a peaceful group. Some of them even look a little like us. One's skin is brown and eyes are dark. Others are white but live in peace with the others. There is a black woman with them but she lives as an equal with the others. I didn't know that different people could live together without fighting. I say we can learn from them."

The young man who spoke first said, "You are always looking for a way out of a fight, Owl. I say we kill them or drive them away. We are the true people of these mountains and do not have to live with ones of different color."

Owl replied, "Running Wolf, you are always looking for a fight and trust no one. The other nations talk of these others that are coming and there is no way to push them back. There are too many. We must learn to live with them or we will soon be looking for a new land to live in."

An older man stepped out beside Tyler, causing him to jump. He hadn't seen him standing beside him.

Running Wolf laughed and said, "Bear Killer, you jump every time Light Foot gets close to you. For someone who has killed the mighty bear, you are very nervous."

Owl said, "I have seen Running Wolf scream out like a child when Light Foot steps out beside him."

Running Wolf started to give an angry reply but Light Foot held up his hand and said, "Enough. I think it is time for Bear Killer to decide what we should do with these others. I want you to go down among them and then make a decision. Whatever you decide, that is what our tribe will do."

He turned to look directly at Running Wolf before any anger could come from his mouth. Running Wolf stared back but then looked at Tyler, Bear Killer, and nodded.

Tyler made his way down the mountain and all his senses were alert like he had never felt before. He was aware of all the animals around him and passed by the squirrels and chipmunks and they only watched as he passed without making any noise. Tyler moved to the edge of the clearing and looked out at the scene before him. Men were plowing new fields while others were digging and hauling stumps from the ground to make more room for crops. Women were by the stream washing clothes, talking and laughing as they worked. Children were playing and some were fishing nearby. The people were very different from one another. There were whites, a black woman, a brown woman and children all working together. Tyler smiled and liked what he saw.

He kneeled down and looked to his left and not two feet from him a child stood looking into his eyes

Tyler Hill's Decision

with wide curiosity. Tyler jumped and blushed and thought that this child must be family to Light Foot.

The young boy spoke and asked, "Are you an Indian?"

Tyler looked at his own skin and clothes and finally answered, "I am of the Cherokee nation."

"My papa told me the Cherokee were good Indians but you are the first one I have seen. Is that a real eagle feather in your hair?"

Tyler looked at the long, single braid of hair that fell over his left shoulder and saw the black and white feather tied to his hair.

"Yes, it is, little one. I am Bear Killer."

The young boy's eyes got even bigger as he said, "My name is Billy and that's my mama and papa."

He pointed at a man and woman standing at the edge of a far field. She was giving him a cup of water. She was black and the man was white.

Bear Killer asked, "Your parents are different colors?"

Billy stood up taller and with a proud look said, "Yes, and that's not all. My grandma is as brown as you and she says I am almost all the colors of the world! Have you really killed bears?"

"Yes, Billy, I have but only because they were trying to eat me."

The look on Billy's face made Tyler laugh and the sound caused all the people to stop and look in his direction.

His hand went to the hilt of the knife on his belt as they approached.

Billy said, "Don't be afraid. They won't hurt you."

Tyler looked down at him and said, "I am afraid of no man!"

"I am sorry, Bear Killer. I didn't mean to say I thought you were afraid."

Tyler smiled and put his hand on top of Billy's head.

Billy's dad came up to Tyler with his rifle pointed at Tyler's chest and said, "What are you doing here? We have nothing for you and we don't want any trouble."

"Tyler, Tyler, wake up. I have someone I want you to talk to."

Tyler opened his eyes and realized he had been dreaming. Walter stood over him and held a cell phone out to him.

Tyler took it and said, "Hello?"

Tyler's mom and then his dad shouted into the phone, so relieved to hear his voice. They talked for a few minutes but the signal was weak. He let them know he was well and that Walter was a good man and helping him get back out of the mountains. His dad said he and Walter had spoken already and his dad wanted to know if Tyler wanted to spend a few more days with Walter. Tyler said in an excited voice that he would like to go to the meeting Walter was going to and he told his dad how much he was learning about the mountains and about the Cherokee people.

He said, "Did you know I am part Cherokee, Dad?"

Tyler Hill's Decision

His dad laughed and said yes, he knew. His papa told him almost every time he visited about that part of him. They talked for a few more minutes and Tyler told his family how much he loved them, something he didn't do very often, and then handed the phone back to Walter. Walter spoke to Tyler's mother and father again for a short time, telling them about when and where they would be able to meet. He closed the cell phone and put it in his small pack.

He said, "I don't get to use this thing very often in the mountains unless I'm near a town. Up here the only way to get a signal is to climb to the top of a mountain, and usually if I do I spend all my time looking out at the world and forget to make a call. I'm glad you didn't mention the bears. That will be a story for when you are back at home with your family. Let's head back down so we don't have to travel in the dark."

They started back down the mountain in the same fashion as they went up, switching trails often. Walter spoke more about the trees and wildlife they saw. Near the base of the mountain Walter stopped and listened and then raised his bow, nocked an arrow in a blur and released all in one motion. A larger rabbit made one leap from under a bush and dropped to the ground.

Walter went to the animal, knelt down for an instance and then field dressed it and removed its fur. He gathered it up and continued to camp. The forest around them was growing dim as the sun settled behind the western mountains when they entered the camp. Walter told Tyler to fill the bucket and cooking pot from the nearby stream and he began preparing the rabbit to cook, rubbing its skin with spices and salt.

They ate all of the small pot of roots, greens and part of the rabbit that was added to a stew. The rest of the rabbit was roasted over the fire and it was consumed by the men and dog.

Tyler asked, "Do you live like this all the time, Walter?"

Walter smiled and said, "As often as I can, but the world we live in demands much of my time so I make sure to set aside some time to be alone in the mountains."

Tyler said, "I'm sorry I have messed up your trip but thank you for finding me and helping me."

Walter looked over at Tyler and smiled, saying, "You sure do apologize a lot and thank me for things that anyone would do in the same situation. I accept your thanks, and know this, Tyler; you are no burden to me. I don't often get to give some of my knowledge to a brother and it pleases me that you found me." Tyler thought about what Walter said for a while. He looked into the flames of the small fire, watching the flames rise up and lick the night and then drop back as if afraid to leave its own kind.

Tyler finally asked, "Why do you call me brother? And is Bear Killer my Indian name?"

Walter laughed and said, "We have the same blood running through us. I may have more of it than you but even a little is enough to be a part of the heritage of the Cherokee people. We don't try to put ourselves above others but at the same time we don't put ourselves below anyone. As to your name, we shall see. In the past, before the others came to our land, the Cherokee used the names of animals and things around them or events so that others would know a little of their story. Now we take the names of Americans and are proud of those names but we still keep our Cherokee names for our brothers and sisters to know us by. For a few days, Tyler, you will live as my brother and then you can decide if this is the name you want to keep.

Tyler said, "I have another name my grandma and grandpa call me but I don't like it very much. They say it is a Thai nickname that Grandma gave me as soon as she saw me."

"What is this name, Bear Killer?"

"It is Taa Paan."

"And what do these words mean?"

Tyler looked a little embarrassed but held his head up and said, "In Thai the words mean *A Thousand Eyes* but it really means Bright Eyes. I don't like it too much and I would never tell any of my friends. They would laugh and tease me even more. I am the only person my grandma ever gave a nickname to. She didn't do it for my dad, uncle or aunt."

Walter smiled and said, "We too have this name and it is for men and women but it is nothing to be ashamed of. It expresses the handsomeness of your face but also the sharpness of your eyes when you hunt or are chased by bears. I think it is a good name for you. What you did without thinking too much when the bears were after you shows that you think and act quickly. It is something to be proud of. Cherokee men have several names and there is no reason for you to give one up for the other. I would like to meet this grandmother of yours one day and see the wisdom she has."

Tyler replied, "I would like that very much. You would like my other grandma, too. She is a strong woman, like my mom, and I enjoy listening to her talk about when Mom was a young girl. She is a good woman."

Tyler lay back on his blanket and looked up at the spreading limbs that covered their campsite. In the firelight the leaves and limbs danced a strange, erratic dance, changing shapes and colors as the flames flared and died back. He picked out shapes of people and animals seeming to run or disappear in an instant. He thought about his parents and family and felt a pang of loneliness. He didn't like not having them around to talk to and he even missed all the advice everyone seemed to want to give to him. He felt like he couldn't do anything right because every time he did something someone was always telling him how he should have done it better. He knew his mom and dad were only trying to help him become a better man but he wanted to learn some things for himself.

He thought about what Walter had said about him being a quick thinker with the bears but he really didn't do a lot of thinking at all. He just moved without stopping to think. He guessed he was just lucky and if it happened again he might be bear food right now. He looked over at Walter, wanting to ask more about the Cherokee, but Walter was sleeping peacefully. He thought about the dream he had had where he was a Cherokee a long time ago and wondered what he would have decided about the settlers. He relaxed and drifted off to sleep.

Chapter 11

###

"Billy, come away from that Indian right now!"

Billy's father's rifle never moved from Bear Killer's chest. Billy was a young boy, around eight or nine years old.

He stepped between his father and Bear Killer and said, "Papa, this is Bear Killer and he is a Cherokee. He's not here to hurt us. I think he just came to meet us."

"Is that right, Indian? Did you just come to meet us?"

Bear Killer slowly reached down with his hand and moved Billy out of the line of fire and said, "I have come to see who is living in the land of the Cherokee. I have not come to make trouble for you or your family."

Bear Killer stood tall and showed no fear of the weapon the man pointed at him.

Billy ran to his father and said, "Please, Papa, don't shoot him. He is my friend and I want him to meet everyone."

Tyler Hill's Decision

Billy's father slowly lowered his rifle but kept a steady eye on Bear Killer.

He said, "If that is true, then you are welcome to come in and meet my family. My name is John Byler."

Slowly he stepped forward and put out his right hand to Bear Killer. Bear Killer grasped John's forearm in the manner of the Cherokee and John's eyes widened for an instant, then gripped Bear Killer's forearm. Neither man had smiled yet but both could feel the other relax a little.

John said, "We have seen Indians passing by a few times when we were out hunting but we never tried to talk to them. We were happy they kept on going and didn't bother us. We've all heard stories about how your people have killed other families here in the mountains."

Bear Killer asked, "What tribe were these people you saw from?"

"I have no idea. They were dressed like you, with feathers in their hair, and several had hair that stuck up in the air like this."

He raised both hands up, spread and pointed his fingers straight up.

Bear Killer said, "They were not Cherokee. They may have been Crow and they shouldn't be on Cherokee land. They live to the north and we have fought them over this land for many years."

John said, "I don't know much about Indians. I thought you were all the same with different names for your villages. We have lived here in this valley for over a year and are trying to make a life for ourselves."

"There are many nations living in these Smoky Mountains. I have heard stories of white men calling us Indians like we are the same people and I have heard stories of whites killing many people to steal their land."

John said, "We have killed no one and we came to the mountains to start a new life and raise our families. We want to live in peace. We didn't know that this land belonged to anyone. Come..." He looked at Billy and asked, "What did you say your friend's name was?"

Billy smiled and said, "Bear Killer. He has killed bears before, Papa."

John looked back at Bear Killer and smiled for the first time and said, "Come, Bear Killer, and meet the others. Please don't raise your weapons or there may be trouble. If you are a friend of my son, then I will speak for you and won't let any harm come to you."

Bear Killer looked steadily at John and said, "I am afraid of no man but I will let you speak for me."

Bear Killer could see four separate homes some twenty yards apart. They were well built, strong and protected by small windows and sturdy shutters. In the center of the houses was an open space with a long table where women were placing food. There were three white women, a black woman and one woman who looked a little similar to one from the tribes but she wasn't.

As John came around the corner of one of the homes he spoke up, "I want you all to meet someone who has come to visit. His name is Bear Killer and he is Cherokee. I have invited him to eat with us."

The women all turned and Bear Killer could see the shock on their faces and the fear. He stood still, with Billy still holding his hand. He did not smile but looked at the women with a steady gaze. All the women except the brown one were young and wore dresses of different colors and bonnets that covered their hair. The brown woman was the first to recover and she smiled and walked out to meet Bear Killer.

"Welcome, Mr. Bear Killer. My name is Sawaan and you are welcome to sit with us and eat."

She looked at John and asked, "Does he speak English?"

Bear Killer answered, "I speak English. A trapper lived with us for several years and he taught me to speak the words of the whites."

The brown woman smiled and said, "I am not white and neither is Doris over there but we speak English."

Bear Killer looked a little embarrassed but only stared at the women.

Amy walked over and said, "Now, Sawaan, don't be embarrassing our guest. Why, pretty soon there will be more people of color than white folks."

The other white woman laughed and walked to meet Bear Killer.

She said, "I am Wynona and I am pleased to meet you. We have seen Indians before but only from a distance. We were told by other settlers that we should be afraid of them and not let them find out we are here. Is that true, Mr. Bear Killer?"

Bear Killer gave them all a steady look through his dark, piercing eyes and could feel the tension.

He relaxed and gave them a small smile and said, "There are some of the nations who do not want *settlers* here and even some of the Cherokee feel that way so you must be wary of people you meet. I am not here to hurt you but only to speak with your men."

Amy asked, "What if you decide you don't like us, sir?"

"I will answer that after I have talked with the men."

Billy called out, "Mama, come meet my friend, Bear Killer." The lone black woman stood off from the others and as she moved toward Bear Killer he could see the frosty looks from the two white women.

She walked over to him and held out her hand and said, "My name is Doris and if you are a friend of my son then you are welcome at my table."

Bear Killer said, "You are black! I have never seen anyone of your color before. How did your skin get so dark?"

Doris was a pretty woman with jet black skin that shone in the sunlight. Her eyes were dark and large and her hair, what he could see of it, was black and coarse. When she smiled her teeth were white and shone like the moon at night.

"I was born like this. I guess you could say my mama and papa gave it to me. I was brought to the colonies as a slave but my master set me free. I came out here with my man but he was killed cutting trees. I belong to John now."

Tyler Hill's Decision

John said, "What she means is she is my woman and I am her man. She is a free woman."

Bear Killer smiled and said, "You must be a good woman to have such a fine boy as Billy. It is good to meet you and all of you as well."

There was a bustling noise from the side of one of the houses and three men rushed around the corner, all carrying rifles. They stopped when they saw Bear Killer and raised the rifles to their shoulders.

John quickly stepped in front of Bear Killer and spoke. "He has come in peace and I have invited him to eat with us. Put your weapons down and come meet our Cherokee neighbor."

One of the men was a giant of a man and he stepped forward a few paces and said, "He comes on our land without permission and you invite him to eat our food? You seem to think anything you do or say is all right."

He then looked directly at Doris with a scowl.

Billy said, "He says we are on his people's land so we might be the ones who are uninvited."

"Shut your mouth and learn some manners, boy, before I teach them to you myself!"

John gave the man a hard look and said, "William, we've had this talk before. Doris and I will take care of teaching Billy what he needs to know. And what he says is true. Bear Killer is here to talk with us about being on Cherokee land."

William said, "This is my land and anyone who tries to take it is in for a fight." He looked at Bear Killer and said, "Do you understand what I just said, Indian?"

"I understand your words. I have come to talk, not fight."

"Well, it's a good thing because I ain't taking no gruff from a little Red Indian."

Bear Killer gave him a hard look but then smiled, thinking that this one will be trouble. Amy ran over to William and spoke softly to him and led him over to the table to eat. The other two men walked over to Bear Killer and offered their hands in friendship. Their names were Wilber and Layton.

Layton said, "Bear Killer, don't mind William. He's a good man but he thinks his size makes him mean. Once he gets to know you he'll be all right. Come and eat with us and then we can talk."

Wilber nodded in agreement and they all went to the table and sat down. Bear Killer saw four other children, two boys about Billy's age, a younger girl and a girl a little older than Billy. They were all white and Billy stayed close to Bear Killer instead of going to sit with the other children.

After eating the men sat under a large oak tree in the shade.

John said, "Bear Killer, will there be trouble between us for having our farms in this valley? We've been here for more than a year and have only seen a few Indians up in the mountains but never here in the valley."

Bear Killer said, "Because you haven't seen us doesn't mean we aren't around. We can go about unseen if we choose. I was sent here to talk to you about this land. After I go back and talk to the council it will be decided what to do."

Tyler Hill's Decision

William started to speak but Layton cut him off. "William, now is not the time to prove how mean you are. The man has come here to talk— so let's talk. Would it be possible to buy this land from you? We don't have much money but we could give something in trade. We didn't come here to steal from another man but to live in peace and to have something of our own."

Bear Killer said, "We have little use for your money but I might ask the council to think about a trade. This is a good valley and we have not lived here for a long time but we do cross here often." He looked directly at William and asked, "Would there be trouble if we were to cross this land if it were yours?"

William said, "I like to know what a man is made of before I trade with him. You look too little for me to fight. Maybe we could see how you are with your weapons."

Bear Killer smiled but it was a cold, unhurried, confident smile and said, "If you would like to see how I use my bow and knife, I will show you, but do not be afraid to fight me. I will not hurt you too much if it is a contest."

John said, "Watch out, William. This man looks like he knows what he is doing."

"All right, little man. Let's have a contest. I'll take it easy on you so you'll be able to walk back to where you came from."

He stood and walked out into the clearing, calling the women over to watch. He always liked to show everyone why he is the leader, even though he was the only one who thought of him like that.

John said, "Bear Killer, you don't have to fight him. He is not our leader and we don't want trouble with the Indians."

Bear Killer looked at John and paused before he spoke. "John, I am a Cherokee of the Cherokee nation. I will fight William. We often have contests of skill among my people and it may help to stop trouble before it starts."

Bear Killer handed his bow, quiver and knife to Billy and walked out into the clearing.

William laughed and said, "Now, when you've had enough you just yell out."

Bear Killer nodded and stood facing William. William rushed at Bear Killer like a great bear with his arms opened wide. Bear Killer waited until William was almost ready to close his arms around him and stepped to the side, brought his right arm over William's outstretched arms and threw his forearm across his neck and left hand in his back to lift William and throw him to the ground. Bear Killer stepped a few paces away as William hit the ground and the air whooshed out of him. William rose to his feet but it took him a moment to catch his breath.

He heard Wilber say, "I guess that's one of the reasons he is called Bear Killer."

William gave him a hard stare and rushed at Bear Killer again. This time he kept his arms in close but out in front, wanting to bowl Bear Killer over. Bear Killer stood upright facing him but just as William reached him he grabbed William's wrists with both hands, dropped down and back and at the same time twisted and lifted his hips. William was again caught off

Tyler Hill's Decision

guard and went flying over Bear Killer, landing on his back. He jumped up and moved slowly towards Bear Killer, wanting to pound the smaller man for embarrassing him. He swung his great fist at Bear Killer's head but Bear Killer ducked and moved to the side. William swung his other arm, with the same results.

He was angry now and yelled, "You're pretty quick for a little man but when I do hit you, you won't get back up, Indian."

Bear Killer stood straight as William moved back in. William swung an upper cut and hit Bear Killer square in the stomach, lifting him off the ground and moving him backwards several feet. William had a pleased look on his face until he saw Bear Killer was still standing, smiling back at him. William knew that that punch should have put any man down but it didn't seem to faze the Indian. He moved quickly in on Bear Killer but when he swung at Bear Killer he felt a punch in his stomach that felt like a mule had kicked him and then Bear Killer's left arm was wrapped around his neck, squeezing so tight that he could not breathe.

William looked straight ahead at the sky and wondered why he was lying on the ground. Amy was kneeling over him and stroking his hair.

He asked, "What happened?"

Amy said, "I think you lost the contest, William."

William sat up and felt a pain in his stomach where something hard had hit him.

He asked John, "What did he hit me with?"

John smiled and said, "He only used his fist, William, and then got you in a chokehold until you passed out."

Bear Killer walked over to William and offered him his hand. William took it and Bear Killer lifted him to his feet like he was a child.

Bear Killer asked, "Would you like to see me use my weapons now?"

William took a deep breath and studied Bear Killer.

He finally smiled and said, "No. I think I've had enough lessons for today. You are a strong man and I want to apologize for being rude. Seeing an Indian— I mean Cherokee— kind of startled me. You are welcome here any time."

Billy said, "I want to see you use your bow, Bear Killer!"

Bear Killer smiled and said, "I will need some help. How about you and," he looked around and continued, "Light Foot helping me."

William asked, "Who is Light Foot?"

A voice right beside William spoke out, causing William to shout in surprise and jump to the side, "I am Light Foot."

Everyone except Bear Killer jumped at his voice and Bear Killer laughed, saying, "Don't be embarrassed. He does that to me all the time."

Light Foot was an older man with dark skin with a reddish tint to it. He had long black hair and a pleasant smile. He was a little taller than Bear Killer and he motioned for Billy to follow him. They went to gather some firewood stacked near one of the homes.

Tyler Hill's Decision

Layton asked, "How long has he been here? I never saw him until he was standing there."

Bear Killer laughed again and said, "That's why he is called Light Foot. He can sneak up on anyone except his wife and we tell him that is why he married her."

They all laughed as Bear Killer strung his bow.

Light Foot and Billy placed pieces of firewood out in the field about forty yards away and then Light Foot told Billy to join the others. He picked up one of the pieces and stepped a few feet away. Bear Killer was ready and as soon as Billy got back and turned around to watch he pulled an arrow from his quiver, nocked it, pulled and released. Then without seeming to stop he continued to pull and release arrows, each one flying to its target and knocking over the pieces of wood. When they were all lying on the ground Light Foot threw the last piece high into the air. Bear Killer released an arrow and it flew straight to the twirling piece of wood and Light Foot caught it before it hit the ground. There was complete silence for a few moments and then they all started to clap.

William said, "Bear Killer, I have never seen anything like that! I think we need to be friends. I wouldn't want to be against you in a fight."

That was exactly what Bear Killer wanted from his demonstration. He could see that these were hard-working people and he had decided as soon as he met Billy that he would tell the party that waited to leave them in peace.

Bear Killer and Light Foot prepared to leave and Billy stayed close to Bear Killer.

John, Billy's father, walked over to Bear Killer and said, "Thank you for taking an interest in Billy. We work hard here and the other children aren't too friendly with him."

Bear Killer asked, "Why would they not be friendly to a fine boy like Billy?"

John pulled Bear Killer away from the others and quietly said, "He is half black. Most whites don't want their blood to be mixed, and if it is, many don't want the mixed people around. With Doris as my wife, we can never return to the East and expect to be left in peace. My first wife died on the journey here and we found Doris all alone in the wilderness. Her husband had been killed trying to build a cabin so we took her in. We fell in love and at first it was difficult, especially for William to accept, but we needed one another to help protect our families so the others have accepted us here. The children are different. The boys tease Billy and he is unhappy because he is not big enough to stand up for himself."

Bear Killer nodded and said he would think on what he has been told. Light Foot and Bear Killer made their way into the forest and were soon out of sight.

###

Chapter 12

Tyler awoke to the sounds of the first birds of the morning singing to the new day. He looked up and watched the light grow, changing his dark tent to the green leaves and needles of the limbs above. He heard Walter get up to start a fire and got up to join him.

Walter said, "Good Morning, Tyler. Did you sleep well?"

Tyler said, "I had the strangest dream. It was almost like it was real."

Walter said, "These mountains will bring out dreams. We will discuss your dreams in a few days. Now help me fix some breakfast and then we will get started."

They started off at a slow pace and Walter continued explaining the things they saw. He stopped at a Sassafras tree and dug out a root and cut a piece off. He split it and handed half to Tyler. It had a sweet smell that was almost like cinnamon and in Tyler's mind he saw steep tree-covered mountains. Walter told him that you could make a tea from the dried roots and chew small pieces but it took some getting used to. The smell was invigorating.

They continued down the valley and the going was easy.

Tyler asked Walter, "Why does no one live in this valley? It seems like a beautiful place to live and be a farmer."

Walter said, "I agree this is a beautiful place and the soil is fertile but it is a closed valley. Both ends are sealed by the mountains. We are two days' walk to the nearest people and there are no roads. You could live your whole life here, growing what you need and hunting. It would be a good life but a lonely life. This is part of Cherokee land and the council has decided not to sell it. There were settlers here many years ago and they were friends of the Cherokee but a war party of Crows came in when the Americans were fighting the British and almost everyone was killed. No one has lived here since then."

They stopped along the stream for a lunch of dried venison, biscuits and honey. Where they stopped, the valley had changed to a forest of tall pine trees. The floor was covered in a thick carpet of pine needles and they made no sound while they walked.

Walter took Tyler to a clearing and they cut a large bundle of tall grass from the glade and Walter used a few stalks to tie the thick bundle together. He placed the bundle in the middle of the glade and turned to Tyler and asked, "Would you like to learn to shoot a bow and arrow?"

Tyler smiled and answered, "My papa has let me try a few times but his bow doesn't look anything like

Tyler Hill's Decision

yours. It has wheels and cables and it is easy to pull back."

Walter said, "A compound bow is a fine weapon, but if it breaks out here, there are no stores to buy parts."

He held up his long, curved bow, stepped through the bowstring and bow and then bent the bow until he could attach the end of the string to the tip of the bow.

"This is called a recurve bow because it curves in and then near the tip it curves out. It is a good bow but it takes a strong, steady hand to use it well."

They were about twenty yards from the grass bundle and Walter pulled an arrow from his quiver and nocked it to the bowstring. He took his time so Tyler could follow what he was doing. He raised the bow and pulled back using his index and middle fingers. When the tip of his middle finger touched the corner of his mouth he released and the arrow flew to the grass target. Tyler was watching closely and saw how Walter's motion was so fluid it reminded him of the water flowing through the stream.

Walter handed the bow to Tyler and Tyler said, "I have never shot a bow like this."

Walter said, "Pull the bow string, point the arrow and let it fly. Give it a try."

Tyler pulled back on the bowstring and felt the strength it took to pull it. He nocked an arrow and prepared to shoot. He took his stance, raised the bow and pulled back. He expected the pressure to ease, like his father's bow, but it took more and more strength to pull it all the way back. Then he tried to aim and he felt his arms begin to shake a little. He proceeded to fight the pressure and aim and finally released the arrow. It flew wide of the target and Tyler felt his face heat in embarrassment.

Walter laughed but put his hand on Tyler's shoulder and said, "Not bad for your first try. This is a strong bow and it takes a lot of practice to build your strength. You are still a young man but with a little practice you will be able to do well."

Tyler tried a few more times and each time the arrow flew farther away from the target. The ends of his fingers on his right hand were aching from where the bowstring had lain in the first joints. His left forearm stung from the bowstring slapping it when he released the arrow.

They cleaned up their camp and moved out down the valley at a slow pace. While they walked Walter talked to him about shooting the bow and how he set the target into his mind. Tyler listened and he felt the stiffness in his shoulder and the hurt of his fingers.

He asked, "How long does it take to be a good shot with a bow like that and how long does it take before my fingers stop hurting?"

Walter said, "You have a natural ability for the bow. I could see it in you when we met, but it takes time to build your muscles. It takes even longer to strengthen your fingers but I have something that will help."

He pulled two pieces of leather from his pack and handed them to Tyler. One piece was small with a large hole and two strips with pouches sewn into the tips. The other was a flat piece of leather with thongs at both ends. Walter showed him how to put his thumb through the hole in the small piece and his fore and middle fingers in the pouches. Then he tied the flat leather to the inside of Tyler's left forearm.

He said, "This will help the pain. Once your strength builds up you will be able to take the finger guard off. If you shoot often, then it is a good idea to wear the forearm piece."

They continued to walk and Walter spoke of hitting the target. He told Tyler that by the time he is at full draw he lets the target pass through his sight line and then releases. He told him if he tried to hold the target he would miss every time.

They stopped early that day and set up another target. Tyler had listened carefully to Walter and on his second shot he hit the target. He shouted with victory at his success. Tyler shot many more times, hitting the target often. By the end of the hour of practice he could barely draw the bow back. Walter laughed and said that was enough for today.

"It is time to find some dinner to cook."

He took the bow from Tyler and they walked into the woods near the camp. Near a clump of bushes he stopped and knelt down.

He spoke softly to Tyler, "Do you see it?"

Tyler looked hard into the bushes but he could only see the limbs and leaves.

Walter said, "Don't look straight at the bushes but move your vision a little to one side and try to see movement."

Tyler did as he was instructed but could see nothing. Suddenly something caught his attention but when he turned his head he saw nothing. He looked away and he caught the movement again. He slowly turned his head and realized he was looking at a rabbit chewing on shoots of grass just at the edge of the bushes. He looked at Walter and nodded. Walter handed him the bow and nodded towards the rabbit. He used his forefinger and pointed at his head and then sliced down in a quick motion. Tyler nocked the arrow, stood, drew the bowstring and released all in one motion. The arrow flew true and took the rabbit through the body. It flopped on the ground but was unable to run.

They walked up to the struggling rabbit and Walter said, "This will be your first kill. Lift it up by its hind legs and with the blade of your hand chop it at the base of its skull.

Tyler timidly lifted the animal and chopped it lightly.

It still struggled and Walter said, "It is in great pain, Tyler, and you must do your job to take the pain away. We take this rabbit to feed us and he gives his body to us for that reason so help it with its pain."

Tyler chopped the rabbit at the base of the skull with a strong stroke and the rabbit stopped moving.

"Good! Now clean it. I will tell you how."

With Walter instructing, Tyler completed the task but he didn't enjoy it. Walter knelt beside Tyler and thanked the rabbit for giving itself to them.

As they walked back to camp Walter talked about the killing of the animals of the forest.

"We kill only to provide for ourselves, not for enjoyment. You should not feel great joy at taking the life of an animal but give it the respect it is due. It is providing for you. If you kill it then you should use it. Many hunters today hunt deer only for their antlers and it makes me sad. If you become a hunter, Tyler, then I hope you will think about my words. Provide for your family and take no more than you will use."

Tyler said, "I didn't really enjoy killing the rabbit. At first I was happy with my shot, but when I saw what I had done it made me a little sad."

"That is as it should be. A true hunter feels regret at killing a beautiful animal but he is also thankful to it for what it will provide."

That night Tyler savored the flavor of his meal and as they relaxed he said, "Walter, I think I will be a hunter, but I will always remember your words. Will you teach me to track?"

"That's one of the reasons you are with me, Bear Killer. We have several days before we reach the meeting place and I will teach you what I can in that time. Tomorrow we leave the valley and cross the western mountains and we will see many beautiful things."

Walter looked over at Tyler and decided it was time to talk of something else. "Bear Killer, you told me that your friends and others sometimes give you a hard time. Tell me about that." Tyler was enjoying the evening with Walter and he didn't really want to talk about those things, but Walter had done so much for him already.

He said, "For a while now some of the kids I know have been teasing me about who I am; I mean because my family is so different from most. I have thought about it too and don't know what I am exactly. Am I African American, white or Asian?"

Walter said "Don't forget about Cherokee as well."

"And Cherokee. Why do I have to be so different? It would be so much easier if I were just one kind of people and I've been thinking about it a lot. I don't want people to tease me and I don't want to hurt part of my family by claiming to be only one."

"How does your family treat you?"

"They're my family. They all love me. When I'm around my grandma of my dad she teaches me Thai ways of doing things. My grandma from my mom treats me like I'm all black and tells me about her life when she was growing up. She wants me to be proud of who I am. My mom and dad just treat me like their son. My grandpa from my dad treats me the same way, except he teases me and likes to hear me laugh. He talks about Thai history and tells me I should be proud to be a part of that people, and he talks about my Indian blood. I don't think he knows a lot about the Cherokee but I know he is proud that he has a little of your blood in him. He told me when he was a little boy that no one in the family would talk about it and he couldn't understand why. He would tell everyone he met that he was part Indian and it seemed to embarrass his family. He says now he understands that people looked down on others who were part Indian and called them half-breeds but he didn't care. He even got into a few fights because someone would say something mean to him about being part Indian, but he found out just being proud was better than fighting.

Tyler Hill's Decision

He also tells me to be proud of my black heritage and that I should keep the best of all of them."

Walter said, "Your family sounds like good people and I could tell by talking to your mom and dad that they love you and worry about you. When I was a child, being a Cherokee was looked down on by many people, mostly whites but blacks and others too. I grew up in these mountains and I could never understand why anyone would look down on me because of who I am. As I grew up and went to work away from here, I would hear all the Indian jokes and even felt the anger of some people. I fought a couple of times but it wasn't worth it. My grandfather always told me to be proud and do what is right. He told me if I did the best I could at everything I did, then people would respect me for that. You know, Tyler, he was right. Oh, I still get teased a little but it is almost always in a friendly way. I have educated many of my friends in the ways of the Cherokee and you might be surprised at how interested they are. They watched all the TV programs about how terrible and bloodthirsty the nations were, and in school it was never taught how badly the nations were treated and tricked by the settlers and government. I have decided that people can think what they want about me, but I will live a good life and from that they can decide what kind of person I am."

Walter paused for a moment, bringing his thoughts back to Tyler. In the few days he had known him he could see the strength and pride of his family in him. He was a young man who could do a lot with his life and he just needed some encouragement. It pleased him that Tyler was with him and giving him an opportunity to share some of his knowledge.

"Tyler, I can't tell you how to make a choice about your background, but you should be proud of all your family and what they have imparted to you. You are filled with many heritages and each one has something to offer you. Take the good in them all and apply them to your life and you will be a special man. You could claim to be only one and maybe sometimes that's okay when you are with certain groups but that is your choice to make. I told you before that even though you only have a little Cherokee blood in you, you are Cherokee. Not all of the people agree with that but I do and you are my brother. You will be welcomed any time you need to come back. I, Light Foot, call you my friend, Bear Killer. Now it is time to sleep."

Walter moved to his bedding and was asleep in only moments. Tyler wrapped himself in his blanket and thought about what Walter had said. He wanted to be a good man and wanted people to respect him for himself. He thought about what it would be like to grow up as a Cherokee. His eyes closed and he drifted off to sleep.

Chapter 13

###

Running Deer and the others waited for Bear Killer and Light Foot to return. He heard Bear Killer making his way quietly up the mountain and looked around for Light Foot.

As Bear Killer came into view, a voice directly behind Running Deer said, "We are back."

Running Deer jumped and darkened. "Do you have to do that every time, Light Foot?"

The others chuckled softly.

Bear Killer said, "I have decided that we are to let the people stay here and I will talk to the council about the land they live on. We can decide what payment will be fair and I will go back to them."

Running Deer said, "It is your decision but we cannot speak for the other tribes and nations. This area is in our hunting grounds but it is far from the villages. Who will protect them if they are allowed to stay?"

"They will have to protect themselves and we can help watch over them when we are in the area. It might be good for us to learn of their ways. I think there will be more people coming here and the valley would be a good place to let them settle. We cannot let them make their homes and cut our forest wherever they want. Maybe this would keep a peace with them. If we fight now, we could easily kill them all, but more are coming and a war with the whites would weaken us against our enemies to the north."

At the council the chiefs listened to all that Bear Killer had to say. One hunter spoke against this idea. In the end it was agreed to let the settlers stay but they must protect themselves. The Cherokee would come to visit and learn some of their ways and try to teach them their own ways. Bear Killer was given the responsibility of collecting the payment for the land and explaining some of the Cherokee customs and laws. He must also warn them that if they broke the laws of the nation they would receive the same punishment.

As Light Foot and Bear Killer entered the clearing near the homes of the settlers they could tell that there was trouble. They moved quietly around one of the homes. They saw the whole group standing around two boys who were sitting on the ground.

William was talking in a very loud voice. "Your boy needs to learn his place. He is mixed and will never make it in this land if he doesn't learn. My boy was just teaching him a lesson for giving him backtalk. At least Doris knows her place."

John was red faced but trying to control his anger. "William, you talk like a fool! We are in the wilderness and have to depend on one another to survive. There is no room for hate or thinking someone is better than another. That's the very reason that most of us moved here in the first place. It might not be normal back in the towns to the east but I love Doris and my son and I won't allow anyone to treat them like they are less than the others here. I can't stop kids from fighting, but I think it is you who needs to teach Amos some manners."

William turned red with anger, pulled his knife and moved in towards John, but before he had moved two feet a knife was at his throat. He stopped, frozen in place with sweat popping out on his forehead.

Doris moved in front of William, keeping the blade against his throat. "I've listened to all your mean words since I was taken in and tried to ignore the hurtful things you and others have said. You can say what you like about me. Yes, I was a slave but now I am a free woman. I am John's wife and he is my husband and we want to live our lives in peace, but if you come at my man again with a weapon, I can't promise you'll come out the other end in one piece. I know how you feel. We all know how you feel. You let us all know what you think every day. And I know it's just your way but, William, I'm getting pretty tired of hearing it. My boy is no different from yours. We are all there is to protect one another and it's time you found something else to complain about. Now, are you calm enough to put your knife away?"

William slowly put his knife back in his sheath and stepped back, looking down at the little woman who he had never seen angry before.

"Doris... I've never seen you like this. I guess I let my words get away from me. We do need everyone here to make this work and I will think about what you have said."

A voice close beside William said, "That is a good idea." William already shaken by having a blade at his throat, jumped and came close to shouting out in fright. He turned and looked into the black, deadly eyes of Light Foot.

"I wish you wouldn't do that!"

Bear Killer stepped up behind William and said, "You just have to get used to it, William."

William jumped again and turned to look into the hard stare of Bear Killer. His shoulders slumped and he turned and walked to a bench and sat down, shaking his head.

Billy jumped up and ran to Bear Killer and hugged his leg. "Hello, Bear Killer. I'm glad you're here!"

Bear Killer lifted Billy's chin and looked at the bruising and bloody nose.

He said, "Looks like someone has been giving you some fighting lessons."

Billy looked over at Amos but said nothing. Amos' left cheek was red and slightly swollen and he had a look of fear in his eyes as he looked back at Bear Killer.

He jumped and shouted in fright as Light Foot stood beside him and said, "I think I will take this one and teach him about the ways of the forest."

"I'm not going anywhere with an Indian!"

Tyler Hill's Decision

William, still sitting down, said, "Shut your mouth, Amos, and say hello to our Cherokee neighbors."

Light Foot put his hand on Amos' shoulder and smiled at him.

John came to Bear Killer and said, "It is good to see you again, Bear Killer. Have you brought us word from your council?"

"Yes. They have agreed to sell you the land you are working and in the future if more settlers come they will also live in this valley. We will sell no land outside this valley."

John smiled, saying, "This is a big valley and will hold a number of settlers but I think it will be a long time before anyone else comes."

Wilber said, "Bear Killer and Light Foot, why don't you join us for our noon meal and we can talk about the price we are to pay."

The women hurried off to prepare a noonday repast. Bear Killer watched the other women hug and smile at Doris as they walked off.

He said, "That is a fine woman you have, John. She would make a good Cherokee woman or maybe even a hunter."

Billy spoke up, "My mama is brave! I never saw her act like that before."

Bear Killer said, "A family must protect one another from anything that comes at them. I think you need a few lessons in fighting as well."

"Will you teach me, Bear Killer?"

"We'll see."

After the meal Bear Killer explained the terms of payment. The settlers thought it was fair as it was mostly paid in bartered goods and free travel rights for the Cherokee. It was decided that one of the men would go with them to the council to make the agreement proper and if they wanted a signed deed then they would have to write it and bring it to the council. The settlers decided that Wilber would go with Bear Killer and Light Foot. Bear Killer talked with William and John for a long time and then William announced that Billy and Amos would be going as well. Billy was excited but Amos didn't like the idea and complained to his father. William told him he was going to learn about how to be a woodsman and a better hunter and he could come back and teach him what he had learned.

They left early the next morning and as they climbed up the mountainside Light Foot spoke to Bear Killer in Cherokee. "These children sound like a herd of moose crashing through the woods. We must quiet them down because we have to pass near Crow territory. I can see the man knows the forest and moves almost like one of us."

After they reached the trail near the top of the mountain, Bear Killer called for a halt and sat with Amos and Billy. He explained the need for quiet and spoke of some techniques to use. He told them that he would walk with Billy and Light Foot would walk with Amos. Amos started to protest but jumped as Light Foot sat down beside him without making a sound.

Bear Killer said, "Amos, wouldn't you like to learn how to do that? There is no better teacher in these

Tyler Hill's Decision

woods than Light Foot. He has taken an interest in you."

Amos said, "I think he just wants to get back at me for beating up Billy."

"No. Challenges are a way of life with the Cherokee. It is a sport and training for our hunters. We treat everyone as an equal, and a challenge must be for good reasons and not made in anger. You should think about why you fought Billy and see if the reason makes any sense. We judge men by their abilities and heart. For now I want you to watch Light Foot and do what he tells you. We are going to pass near Crow territory and it would be dangerous to meet them right now. It is important to learn these things."

Amos said, "I will watch him."

Wilber said, "I'm going to watch as well. He moves like no one I've ever seen."

Bear Killer said, "It will take us three days to reach our village so we will have time to get to know one another. I am glad we have a man like Wilber with us and two strong boys if we have trouble."

They started off again with Light Foot in the lead. Light Foot could speak a little English, but most of his instructions were through his actions and hand signals. Bear Killer used the same method with Billy and within a few hours they were all moving through the forest silently.

They were on a game trail and occasionally they came to an outcrop of rocks that gave them a vista of the valleys and mountains around them. The view looked like a dark green ocean with rock outcrops like islands. There was a constant haze that gave the

Smoky Mountains their name but they could still see for miles. The air was crisp and cool and smelled fresh with a scent of the trees and earth. Bear Killer began to name the trees with their Cherokee names and English names and Billy listened to everything he said. He felt safe being with Bear Killer and his mind cleared from the worries he sometimes had around all the other people. He knew he was different but then again, he didn't feel different until someone made a comment about his father and mother. Bear Killer and Light Foot had never even said anything about his darker skin and dark eyes. He began to feel the freedom of the mountains and it lifted his spirit.

They began to move so quietly that when they passed squirrels and chipmunks they just ignored the men passing by. Light Foot smiled and nodded to Amos, who had begun to enjoy himself. He was having the same feeling of freedom that Billy was beginning to feel. He could see that Light Foot really was interested in him. He never knew the Indians... Cherokee were men just like his father and the other settlers. He had always thought they were wild men and only wanted to kill the settlers and steal from them, or at least that was all he heard.

Light Foot led them to a cliff face and climbed a short way up to a rock ledge. On the ledge they found a large cave with firewood stacked in the back. After they dropped their packs, Light Foot indicated that Amos should follow him and they left the cave. Wilber prepared a small fire and Bear Killer took Billy into the forest to an open glade. At the edge he studied the area and soon found what he was looking for. He pointed and asked Billy what he saw. Billy looked hard but only saw bushes and grass growing in the glade. Bear Killer leaned down and told him to look at the bush he was pointing at and then look away just a little. Billy did what he was told and soon caught movement at the corner of his eye. He slowly moved his eyes and saw two rabbits eating grass under the bush. He nodded to Bear Killer, who moved out into the glade with his bow ready, and as the rabbits sprang from under the bush he released one arrow and then another, killing both rabbits.

As they cleaned the rabbits Billy asked, "Do you think I could ever learn to shoot like that?"

"Yes, if you practice. If you would like, I will help you, Billy, but most settlers have firearms and think the bow is only for us."

"A rifle can only shoot one time and then you have to reload, but with a bow you can shoot many times before a rifle is reloaded."

"I will begin to teach you but this bow is too strong for you and it would hurt your shoulder if you tried to use it. For now I will talk to you about hunting and using the bow. When we get to my village I will make you a bow that will fit your strength."

That night Wilber and Bear Killer sat together talking.

Wilber said, "Not all of us feel like William does about Doris and John. I had trouble at first, but the more I watched them, the more I could see they are good for each other. Billy will grow into a fine man because of the way John and Doris guide him. I came out here to make a life for my family but my wife and son died from sickness so I've been on my own for a while. I also came because of the stories I heard about the Indians. You live with the land and only use what you need of it. The same with the animals; you only take what you need to provide for your village. I like that. I have seen some men kill an entire herd of animals just for the sport of it. Most of the meat and fur was left to rot and it's just not right to treat the gifts of God like that. I would like to learn more about the Cherokee and learn your language as well. Do you think that I might find someone to teach me?"

Bear Killer smiled and said, "I think you will find someone who will teach you our ways. I have watched you as well. I can see you are a strong man with a good heart. I will bring you to the council and tell them what you asked."

Light Foot spoke, making them both jump. "I help too. I teach you as well."

Wilber laughed. "If I can ever learn to sneak around like you do, I will have a lot of fun back in the valley."

The next day they traveled, climbing up a mountain, heading for a cut. At one point Bear Killer stopped them to rest and he went off into the woods. He returned carrying two long, narrow limbs.

He said, "This is from the ash tree and will make good bows. Billy and Amos, you are to carry these and get the feel of them."

As they walked along the game trails Bear Killer and Light Foot would stop and point out the different tracks of the animals that used the trail. There were large prints of bear and wolves, smaller cloven hoof prints of two different kinds of deer and numerous small prints of weasels, minks, skunks, porcupines and large rodents. They would explain how each traveled and how they lived. The two boys and Wilber listened to everything that they said. Bear Killer could see Amos and Billy becoming closer the deeper into the forest they went. They stopped once and picked a sackful of hickory nuts, mushrooms and green leafy plants.

A few hours before sunset Light Foot disappeared but Bear Killer seemed unconcerned. He had them stop near a clear stream and make camp. Amos and Billy gathered wood and when they returned to camp Light Foot was there with a small deer. He was cutting the meat into thin strips and rubbing the meat with a little salt and herbs. He had cut out the back straps and was roasting them over the fire with a green sapling pierced lengthwise through the meat. Wilber was scraping the hide to remove loose pieced meat and fat. They would rub the skin in wood ash after the fire died down.

As they ate the delicious meal both boys looked closely at the staffs of wood they carried.

Amos said, "I never shot a bow before; have you, Billy?"

Billy said, "No, but after watching Bear Killer use one I would like to learn. It would come in handy hunting."

Amos said, "I wonder how Bear Killer got his name."

Billy said, "Why don't you ask him?"

"I don't think he likes me very much. He gives me some hard looks once in a while. But he likes you, Billy. Why don't you ask him?"

Billy turned to Bear Killer and asked. Light Foot laughed and said he would like to hear that story again. So Bear Killer told about being chased by two bears when he was just a little older than Billy. He had spent two days in a tree but the bears wouldn't leave.

Light Foot said, "Bear Killer looked like good meat and bears never pass up food."

Bear Killer continued on with the story of being tricked by the bears to come down from the tree. As soon as he was on the ground they rushed out of the bushes and almost had him, but he ran as fast as he could around the mountain. He saw an outcrop of rocks and ran through the thick bushes. Just as he came out of the bushes he found he was on a flat rock that ended in a drop-off. He couldn't stop and over the edge he went, but luckily there was a small tree growing straight out from the side of the cliff and he landed on it. The tree swung him to the rock face. The bears were so intent on catching him that they followed him over the cliff and fell to their deaths. Bear Killer pulled a necklace out of his buckskin shirt and showed them two large claws. Light Foot laughed again and said that was all that was left of the bears after they fell two hundred feet to the rocks below. Bear Killer laughed and said Light Foot found him hanging on to the cliff and helped him climb back up. It took four hours to get to the bottom of the cliff to find the bears. He and Light Foot have been close friends ever since.

Tyler Hill's Decision

"Even though Light Foot is an old man now, he is still my best friend," said Bear Killer with a smile.

That night before he slept Amos thought about the words of Bear Killer and Light Foot. He would like to have a friend like that, and the more he thought about it, he thought Billy would make a good friend.

###

Chapter 14

The next morning Walter and Tyler were up early, ate a quick breakfast and continued climbing up the mountain. Walter found a large game trail that ran along the slope of the mountain and it made the going easier. He began talking and demonstrating how to move through the forest without making a sound. It was an attitude as well as being careful where he put his feet. They stopped often and Walter talked about the different trees and what could be gathered from them.

"In the winter the white oaks have large acorns that the deer love to eat so they are a good place to hunt."

"Can a person eat the acorns?"

Walter said, "Yes, but they must be soaked many times to take out the tannic acid and they don't have a lot of flavor. Some acorns, like the red oak, are too bitter to eat, but there are many things in the forest that are tasty so leave the oak trees for firewood and building strong homes.

Tyler Hill's Decision

Tyler walked behind Walter and watched him as he moved. In clear areas he walked normal, heel first and then toes, but in leafy, overgrown areas he moved placing his toes first and then his heel. He didn't seem to make any effort in changing his style of walking; it came naturally.

Tyler asked him about that and Walter replied, "It is natural for me now but it took a long time practicing to make it natural. If you want to learn to do this, you must think about every step you take for a while and you must be aware of everything around you as well. It isn't easy to begin with but the more you do it, the less you have to think about it. I remember as a boy everyone would tease me for walking on my toes but I didn't listen to them. I listened to my grandfather and soon I was able to walk up to people without them knowing I was there. I did it as practice but it did become fun, too. The others stopped teasing me. Why don't you walk ahead of me for a while and let me see you try. I will not tease you but I might laugh once in a while. If you can learn to laugh at your mistakes instead of becoming angry, it makes learning much easier, Tyler. Here; you carry my bow and don't forget; you must be aware of everything around you."

Tyler took the lead and concentrated on every step he took, trying hard not to make a sound. He would still break twigs and rustle leaves but as time passed he began to make less noise. He wasn't paying much attention to his surroundings because walking was taking so much concentration. As he rounded a larger hickory tree he nearly stepped on Walter's feet as he sat on a stump by the trail. Tyler jumped and shouted in fright and Walter let out a friendly laugh.

Tyler looked behind him and then asked, "How did you do that?"

Walter only smiled and said, "Practice... now, don't forget to listen and watch your surroundings."

They continued for two more hours and about every ten minutes Walter would be standing beside the path in front of Tyler. It became a game. Tyler once rounded a large oak as quietly as he could and continued on around the trunk to surprise Walter. When he arrived on the trail Walter was nowhere to be seen.

Walter slapped him on the shoulder and said, "I am behind you, Tyler."

Tyler yelled and jumped but then laughed, shaking his head.

Walter said, "Laughing is the first sign of getting better, Bear Killer. I can see much improvement in your style already. Open your mind a little more and try to sense the animals around you as you move. It is another step in learning to be a part of the forest."

They stopped for lunch and ate some jerked venison and cornbread. Walter continued to teach Tyler about the ways of the forest and how the Cherokee lived with nature instead of trying to dominate it. Tyler listened to every word. Watching Walter put his words into practice made the learning fun and exciting.

After eating they began to head down the mountain and Tyler concentrated on not making a sound. He found he could pass close to squirrels and chipmunks without disturbing them. He listened to the forest and found he could hear birds flicking between branches in the trees, looking for food. He heard animals moving through the leaves. He even saw three does moving along a trail below him and he stopped to let them pass by. They never looked in his direction.

They entered another valley much like the one they had traveled through. Here too there seemed to be no one living there. Tyler asked how so much land could be without people and Walter said they were far in the mountains and there were no roads near this area.

He said, "This is one of my favorite places in the mountains because it is still wilderness. If a road were ever built here, it would take away the peace of the mountains."

A few hours before sundown they stopped and Walter made a target for Tyler to continue his practice with the bow. He was hitting the target every time but his arms were soon sore. They camped near a stream that gurgled and whispered as it passed by. They bathed and cleaned the heat of the day off and Walter helped Tyler catch several large trout for their supper. Walter spoke more of heritage and how each one should be part of Tyler's makeup. He spoke of pride in oneself and not letting others dictate how he felt.

"If you take pride in what you do and how you do it, then your character will show through to others. Remember the Bible says to treat others like you would like to be treated. In this modern world we live in it is hard to do. Many people want to be treated special, but a person has to understand his own confidence. That and his family values guide him no matter how others try to treat him. Your friends and peers will often try to test your resolve and it is up to you to laugh with them or ignore some of the mean things they say."

Tyler said, "You have given me a lot to think about, Walter, but I can see I need to start listening more to the people who love me and not to the ones I think are cool. I think I will have many things to say to my parents and family."

Walter smiled and was quiet for a while as he prepared the fish over the open fire.

"Pay attention to who notices these little changes in you first. That will be a good guide to who cares for you."

As they ate, Walter told Tyler about things that happened to him as a child and they laughed at some of the predicaments he got into as a boy. Tyler related a few embarrassing things he had done and found he could laugh about them and the embarrassment went away.

"You know, Walter, I haven't ever gone this long without watching TV or playing video games and I don't miss them. I guess this is what the people did before we had all that stuff."

"You're right, Tyler. People used to talk and tell stories, sing, help their neighbors and go out and see the world around them instead of staying inside their houses with the doors locked. I think people are lonelier now than they have ever been and it's too bad."

As Tyler lay down he listened to the stream rushing over the rocks and it was so much better than the music on his *iPod*. There were no words to disturb him or paint their pictures in his mind. The babbling brook allowed him to paint his own and he soon drifted off to sleep.

#

Amos and Billy were following behind the others as they moved toward the Cherokee village. Amos was trying to get to know Billy, but Billy was wary of Amos. Amos had caused nothing but trouble for Billy and punished him whenever they were away from the adults. Billy was expecting Amos to try something soon. Billy did notice that Amos was not acting like his usual self and he was asking Billy questions about what Billy liked to do.

As they walked they heard a noise at the same time and looked off the trail and saw a fawn moving into a blackberry bush. It was tan with a white belly and still had white spots to camouflage its body. They looked around quickly and tried to see the mother but she was not in sight. Amos waved Billy to follow and he stepped off the trail, heading for the bush where the fawn disappeared. Billy followed but was worried about getting too far behind the others. Amos was so intent on finding the fawn that he paid no attention to anything else.

Billy heard a noise from down the trail they had been on and saw more Indians coming around a bend in the trail about thirty yards behind them. They were not Cherokee. At least they were dressed differently than Bear Killer and Light Foot. There were three of them and they all had arrows nocked to their bowstrings and were moving quietly. Amos turned to speak and Billy put his hand over Amos' mouth and quietly pushed him into the bramble. Amos struggled but Billy used all his strength to hold him down and keep him quiet. He looked into Amos' eyes and Amos could see the fear. He relaxed a little and Billy turned his head toward the Indians coming up the trail. Amos looked and saw the Indians and stiffened in fright. He tried to rise but Billy held him down and shook his head. Amos nodded and put his hand on Billy's and Billy slowly removed his hand from Amos' mouth. They moved further into the bushes and lay flat.

As the Crows came to where Billy and Amos left the trail, one of them stopped and looked at the ground. He turned in the direction that they had gone and looked intently at the blackberry bushes. He held his hand up and the other two stopped. He started in towards where the boys lay.

Billy could feel Amos try to rise but he gripped his arm strongly and held him down. He looked around and saw the fawn, not three feet from where they lay. It was also lying frozen in the bramble and thorns, breathing rapidly but not making a sound. Billy reached out and picked up a dead stick and slowly moved the tip toward the deer. He made a quick, short stab at the fawn and it sprang up and bound out of the bushes.

The Crow stopped at the noise and saw the small deer bounding away through the forest. He turned and the other two men smiled at him. He shrugged and returned to the path. They moved off following the Cherokees and Wilber.

Tyler Hill's Decision

Billy started to move out of the bushes but Amos grabbed him and whispered, "Don't go out there. They might hear you and come back."

Billy whispered, "They are going after our friends and we have to warn them."

"No, Billy! They might kill us."

"I'm not going to let them kill my friends. You can stay here, Amos, but I am going."

Billy moved out of the bushes and looked around the ground. Billy had dropped the staff that Bear Killer had given him when he saw the Crows. He picked up a dead limb from a nearby hickory tree and started off down the trail. Amos, not wanting to be left alone in the forest, picked up another stick and followed but he was very frightened. He watched Billy moving like Light Foot had taught them and he began to follow in Billy's footsteps.

They followed for only a few minutes and as they rounded a bend in the trail they saw the three Crows had stopped and were using hand-signals to plan their attack. Two of the men separated, moving off the trail and up the mountain. The other Crow moved down the trail slowly but suddenly stepped behind a tree. Billy looked and saw Bear Killer coming back down the trail. The Crow pulled back on the bow and was preparing to step out and shoot Bear Killer. Without thinking, Billy ran at the Crow and yelled a warning to Bear Killer. "Watch out, Bear Killer— Indians!"

The Crow jumped at the sound of Billy's voice, turned, and before he could aim his bow, Billy smashed him with the dead limb. The limb shattered and did little damage but it stopped the Crow long enough for

Amos, who was right behind Billy, to hit him with the limb he had picked up. His limb was strong and it connected with the Crow's head. The man dropped like a sack of potatoes. Amos hit him again and Billy grabbed the bow and ran towards Bear Killer. Bear Killer saw that the two boys were all right and running towards him so he turned and raced up the trail, giving a scream that sent chills through the boys. He was warning Light Foot.

When the boys arrived where Light Foot and the others were, they saw one Crow lying on the trail with blood everywhere and they could hear someone crashing through the trees. Wilber sat on the ground with an arrow in his upper arm and bleeding. Light Foot left the trail at a run, following after the Crow but returned in only a few moments. He spoke to Bear Killer as he attended the wound in Wilber's arm. Bear Killer nodded and looked at the boys.

"Light Foot says the Crow will not stop until he is back in his village or he falls off the mountain."

He then spoke to Light Foot and Light Foot ran back down the trail to check on the Crow that Amos and Billy had hit.

Bear Killer was cleaning the wound on Wilber's arm and said, "It is not bad. We will take care of it when we reach the village."

Wilber said, "It's just a scratch. I'll be fine."

Light Foot returned and said, "The other Crow is gone, but without his bow he will be chasing after his friend to see who gets home first."

Tyler Hill's Decision

Billy remembered he was holding the bow and started to hand it to Light Foot but Bear Killer said, "That is yours, Billy. You won it in battle."

Billy turned to Amos and said, "Here, Amos; you are the one who hit him the hardest."

Amos said, "No, Billy. You saved my life back there. If you hadn't kept me from jumping up, we might both be dead right now. That is your bow to keep. You are a lot stronger than I thought." He put his arm around Billy's shoulder and smiled.

Bear Killer stood and walked over to Billy, saying, "I must thank you as well, Billy. If you hadn't yelled and attacked the Crow, he might have killed me also. I will tell my people of how both you young men acted to protect us. You two make good partners."

Billy was embarrassed with the pride he felt and looked at Amos and saw the smile on his face.

For the next two days as they moved Light Foot taught all three of the settlers more about moving through the forest. Bear Killer also spoke of how to live in harmony with the mountains and spoke of hunting and how the Cherokee lived. Amos and Billy were becoming good friends and Amos asked many questions about Billy and his mother. He was surprised to find that they were no different than his family. He told Billy they would be friends and he was sorry for the way he had treated him before. Bear Killer heard these conversations and wondered how people could live so close together and not know each other, but he was learning more about how the settlers thought.

Billy couldn't believe that that one incident could make such a change in his life. He was treated with respect by the entire group and it brought him a happiness he didn't know he could have. He was looking forward to meeting all the people of Bear Killer's village and learning more about the Cherokee. He also couldn't wait to get back to tell his mama and papa about all that had happened.

###

Chapter 15

Tyler awoke to the sounds of the forest. He lay still and listened to the animals begin to forage for food and the birds call to one another. The breeze moving through the branches of the trees and the babbling brook nearby were sounds he was growing to love. He smiled at the word *babbling*. He had read it before but it made no sense to him when coming from a book. Now he understood. The water rushing along the rocky streamed did sound like people talking from a distance. No words were understood but it was a pleasing sound.

He thought about the dreams he had been having of the settlers of these mountains and wondered if things like that really happened. He knew that Billy would have had a much harder life than he did. He had read about life for African-Americans a long time ago. Brought here as slaves and treated as property, he couldn't imagine what that would have been like. He also read about how tribes in Africa captured one another and sold the captives to Arabs and Europeans for trade goods. The world has come a long way since then. There was an African-American who was President and he did a good job.

The dream of Billy and the Cherokee made him think about his own life and the choices he needed to make. He loved his family and thought about how each of them lived their lives. Walter had said he should take the good in his entire heritage and use it in his life, but he still wondered how to answer the question of who he was. He would talk to Walter more about this.

He thought about Walter and smiled. He had never met anyone like him outside his family. He didn't seem to have any prejudice towards anyone and he made up his own mind. Maybe living in the mountains did that to people. It made them strong and independent and probably lonely too. He wasn't sure if he would like being alone so much but he guessed he could get used to it if he tried.

Tyler got up and moved over to the fire and did like he had watched Walter do. He stirred the ashes and saw a few sparks, bent over them and blew softly. He added a few small pieces of wood and the flames leaped to life. He added more wood and then went to the stream to clean up. He saw several nice-sized fish swimming in a small pool by the edge and lay on the ground and slowly lowered his hands into the water. Just like before, the fish came into his hands and he softly stroked them. He soon had two fish on the bank. As he walked back into the camp Walter was near the fire, heating water and cooking flatbread.

Tyler Hill's Decision

He looked up and smiled at Tyler and said, "You are becoming quite a woodsman. I think soon you will teach me a thing or two."

Tyler laughed and said, "I think I would have to be here a long time to teach you something new, Walter."

After they ate they started off down the valley with Tyler in the lead again. As he walked it became much easier to walk quietly and to place his feet along the trail. Tyler found he didn't need to think about every step and had a chance to look around at the ever-changing forest. There were white barked beech, shaggy barked hickory, massive oaks and stands of tall pines. They passed through glades of grass and flowers and he saw where the deer had bedded down for the night. After a while Walter began to show him tracks and signs and explained how to tell how old they were and a little about what the animals might have been doing. It amazed Tyler that he could glean so much information from just looking at the tracks of the animals.

Near noon Walter put his hand on Tyler's shoulder to stop him. He pointed to a raspberry bush and asked if Tyler saw the tiny bird flittering among the branches. Tyler had to look hard but then he saw the small yellow bird busily hopping through the bush. Walter said it was a bee-eater and he walked to the bush and softly whistled. The bird stopped and seemed to look at Walter and then began to sing and flew to a nearby limb, turned and waited. It was singing excitedly.

Walter said, "Our little friend will lead us to a very sweet treat but we must follow quickly because it will be very excited to lead us."

Walter took the lead and moved swiftly through the forest. He would whistle and the tiny bird would answer and fly ahead. After about twenty minutes it stopped and its sound changed to an excited trill. Walter and Tyler stopped and looked around. Walter pointed up into a water oak tree and Tyler could see what looked like smoke hovering by the trunk about twenty feet off the ground. As he looked closer he could see a swarm of bees flying in and out of a large hole where a big branch had broken off years before.

Walter smiled and said, "Now we're in for a treat. Help me gather some dried leaves and I will find some green grass." After they gathered a substantial pile of leaves and grass Walter wrapped the dried leaves and grass around a small dead limb.

Tyler asked, "Are you going up there? Won't they sting you?"

Walter smiled, "I might get stung a few times but it will be worth it. The smoke will calm the bees and they will let me gather some of their sweet food but I can't take it all."

He climbed to just below the opening and lit the leaves. They caught quickly and then as the green grass started to smolder it made a thick, white smoke. Walter, careful to keep the burning stick away from the bees, began to blow the smoke into the hole. As Tyler watched, the cloud of bees began to dissipate and he could see them settling on the trunk and making their way into the opening. Walter reached into the opening with his bare hand and Tyler could see his arm moving. Soon he came out with a white pie-shaped disk and put it in his pouch. He reached in once more and removed a smaller disk that was much darker than the first. He brushed the bees off the comb with his hand. He blew a little more smoke into the hole and then made his way down to the ground. The whole time he worked the little bird sang sweetly as if to encourage him, but now as Walter reached the ground the bird went still.

Tyler asked Walter, "Why has the bird gone so quiet?"

Walter replied, "He is waiting for his share."

They moved away from the tree a short distance and Walter pulled some green oak leaves from a tree and placed them on the ground. He reached into his pack and removed the small disk of wax. Tyler could see the cells of the comb and some were closed over with a white cap but others were packed with a dark yellow material. Still others had what looked like small white wiggling worms in them. Walter explained that this was where the queen laid her eggs and that the worms were young bees.

"The bee-eater loves the young ones and the dark pollen as much as the honey." He laid the small comb on the leaves and said, "Thank you, my friend, for your help. Please enjoy the fruits of your labor."

The small bird fidgeted but remained silent until they moved away and then it launched itself at the comb. Tyler laughed and wondered how it could sing and eat at the same time.

They moved back to the trail and sat near the stream to eat lunch. Tyler had only seen honey in a jar but he recognized the comb filled with the sweet, sticky, golden liquid. As they ate the delicious offering, Walter explained that you should only take a little of the honey and leave most of it for the bees so they would make more and stay in the tree.

He also talked about the bird, saying, "The bee-eater has always helped the Cherokee to find the hives and we know that we must always give them their share. Once, long ago, one of the braves did not give any honey to the bee-eater and it became angry. It waited for a long time for its revenge but one day it saw the brave and began its honey song. The brave followed the bird to a cave where the bee-eater waited by the entrance to show him where his treat was. The brave made his smoke stick and moved into the cave and found a huge black bear sleeping. The fire startled the bear and he became enraged and killed the brave. The bee-eater flew away singing a happy song and was never tricked again by the Cherokee."

Tyler looked at Walter and asked, "Is that really true?"

"It is one of the many stories of our people, but true or not, I would never trick the bee-eater to find out."

As they walked in the afternoon they came upon a wide meadow of grass and wildflowers. Walter named many of the flowers in the field and explained what they could be used for. There were the Meadow Rue with its tiny cluster of white flowers and soft round leaves, Spiked Lobelia with blue downturned flowers growing one on top of the other on a thick stalk, wild Columbines with red tinted flowers with a king's crown shape on top of the flower, and Goldenrods with long, spiked leaves and yellow flowers were in profusion. Primrose, Toothwort and Brown-Eyed Susan were all scattered in the field of color. All the colors of the rainbow opened before Tyler's eyes and he tried hard to remember their names. It would be something for him to study when he got back home. He could see that a person could spend a lifetime in the Appalachians and never see all the beauty that was there. He wished he had paper and pen to write it all down. He wanted his family to share this experience with him.

As Tyler listened and talked with Walter, he thought of the background of his family that gave him all the different pieces to his makeup. The differences didn't seem as big as he looked up the tree-covered slopes of the mountains. He was a young man and he thought he was a good person. Walter talked to him like an equal and only spoke of his heritage in positive ways. It just didn't seem important, but he knew when he got back the questions would begin again, although he really didn't understand why.

As they walked through the field of swaying grass and wildflowers, Walter stopped and handed his bow and quiver to Tyler.

He said, "It's time you earned your keep, Tyler. See that bramble of blackberries near the edge of the field? There should be a few rabbits in there and we need some meat for supper."

Tyler looked at Walter and said, "You want me to go on my own?"

Walter laughed as he spoke. "You can do this, Tyler, but I want to make one thing clear. Don't bring back any bear! I'm not that hungry."

They both laughed at that and as Tyler walked off he felt a sense of pride at the responsibility he had been given.

Walter called after him, "Bring back some blackberries, too. They will give a good flavor to the meat."

Tyler moved the way Walter had shown him and as he glided through the field he didn't make a sound or any quick movements. Walter watched him with a sense of pride and looked forward to introducing Tyler to his friends at the gathering.

Tyler moved to within twenty feet of the bushes and kneeled down to slowly scan the area. After only a few minutes he saw a rabbit move to the edge of the bushes and look around. It was soon munching on the tender grass under the bushes. Tyler shot from a kneeling position and the arrow passed through the rabbit. Tyler nocked another arrow and before he moved to pick up his game another rabbit came out to see what happened. It saw Tyler move and took off out into the field. Tyler led his target and brought the second rabbit down. He thanked them for their gift of life and cleaned them. He gathered a small pouch of ripe blackberries and started towards the slope where Walter was setting up camp.

Walter and Tyler made camp high up on a mountain slope under a rock overhang. Sitting at the

Tyler Hill's Decision

edge of the drop-off they could look far down the slope into the valley they had been walking.

Tyler said, "That was the best meal I've had in a long time, Walter. I never thought rabbit and blackberries could be so good."

"I rubbed it with a little sage, salt, wild basil and blackberry juice and then stuffed it with the berries. You provided the meat and all I did was add a little flavor."

Walter continued, "Tell me a little more about your grandpa. He's old enough to have grown up when whites and blacks lived differently."

"My grandpa told me that he never understood why so many people hated each other just because of the color of their skin. He said his friends were always making bad jokes about black people and he even admitted to making some as well just to fit in. He told me a story about going into the city with his mom and they rode the bus. He remembered looking in the back of the bus at the black people and thought they were lucky to get to look out the back window. He started to get up and go to the back to sit but his mom stopped him. She said, 'If you go to the back of the bus the black people will have to stand because they can't sit in front of a white person.' He asked her why and she would only say that that's the way it is."

"He said it bothered him a lot but he was just a kid and didn't understand that it was a sign of disrespect. Grandpa told me he was glad when the laws were changed but it really didn't change society. He told me he was happy that we had a young man in the family who could stand up and take a stance in almost any situation and he would be there to back me up."

Tyler thought for a minute and said, "My grandpa also tells me that people from other lands always fascinated him when he was a kid. He said he met a man from Italy once and it was exciting. I laughed because Italy is just over in Europe."

Walter smiled and said, "I think your grandpa and I are a lot alike in the way we look at things. Maybe I'll have to meet him some day."

"I hope you will get to meet my whole family, Light Foot. I would be proud for them to meet a friend of mine."

Tyler wrapped himself in his blanket and soon fell asleep.

Chapter 16

###

The small party entered the Cherokee village and Billy was looking around everywhere. The houses were made of small pine logs and thin limbs woven together into a lattice. The walls were filled in with mud and the roofs were thatched with pine boughs. There were only a few windows and a single small door in each house. They were not set up in an orderly fashion but most faced toward the center where there was a large cleared area. The paths were clean and there were people and dogs everywhere.

As they walked to the center of the village many people came out to look at them. There were no smiles and a few hard looks. Some children looked at them with curiosity and the larger boys with anger. Billy was glad he walked with Bear Killer and Light Foot.

A group of older men sat on logs around a fire and as Bear Killer walked up one of the oldest men stood. He was not tall and had skin that looked like dark tanned leather but his eyes had a piercing, intelligent look as he surveyed the visitors. Bear Killer motioned for the settlers to sit and wait and then he approached the old man.

Bear Killer said, "Two Feathers, I have brought some of the settlers to speak about the land where they live and to see our village."

"The decision has been made about the valley. There is no need to bring anyone to our village."

Bear Killer said, "I have found that these are good people and the youngest boy is in need of friendship. He is different from the others and is a brave young man."

"How do you know he is brave?"

"We were attacked by Crow on the journey here and all three whites helped. The young one attacked a Crow that was about to shoot me. He only had a stick but he faced the Crow. The other boy finished the Crow off. The man fought and was wounded. Light Foot killed one and the other two escaped."

Two Feathers turned to the settlers and spoke to Billy.

Bear Killer translated. "This is Two Feathers. He is our chief and he asked you, Billy, why did you attack the Crow." Billy looked around at all the hard faces that waited for him to answer. He stepped closer to Amos for assurance and Amos put his hand on Billy's shoulder for support.

"I only wanted to help my friend, Bear Killer. My stick broke and Amos is the one who hit the man hard."

Amos said, "If Billy hadn't attacked him, he would have shot Bear Killer with an arrow. I just followed Billy and helped."

~ 127 ~

Tyler Hill's Decision

Bear Killer translated what the boys had said and Two Feathers said, "I am pleased to hear you call Bear Killer your friend. All of you are welcome and we will see about teaching you more about the Cherokee and maybe you can learn to speak our language."

Billy, Amos and Wilber stayed in the village for a week and learned much about the Cherokee way of life. The boys were accepted by the other children and many wanted to have them as friends. Wilber met a woman about his age named Indulala, which meant *Moonlight*. She offered to teach him her language and they soon became good friends.

Later Wilber would visit the village often and took Indulala as his wife. She stayed in the valley, helping everyone learn more about the Cherokee way of life.

Amos and Billy became lifelong friends. William, Amos' father, became a favorite at the village and he was often invited to show his great strength.

Many Cherokee came to the valley to see the dark-skinned woman, Billy's mother, and she had a special place in their hearts.

###

Chapter 17

Tyler and Walter walked into the meeting place and Tyler stayed close to Walter.

A man named Ben came out to meet Walter and said, "Ho, Light Foot. It has been many weeks since we last saw you. I see you have found a bear cub in the mountains." He smiled and moved to Tyler, saying, "I am Ben Walking Deer and I am happy to meet a friend of Light Foot's. I hope you don't move around like Walter. He scares at least two or three people during his visits by sneaking up on them."

"Hello. My name is Tyler Taa Paan Hill, and Walter has been teaching me how to move in the forest."

Walter said, "Tyler has another name as well. He is called Bear Killer."

Ben looked at Tyler in surprise and asked, "How did you come to get that name?"

Walter laughed and said, "That is a story for the fire tonight but it will be worth the wait."

Tyler Hill's Decision

Many of the people came to greet Walter and meet Tyler. They made Tyler feel like part of their family and it made him miss his own family.

Tyler tried to stay close to Walter but soon many of the children pulled him away to play and see the things they had made. Tyler was too busy to be lonely.

That night there was a gathering around a large campfire and the people were waiting for Ben Walking Deer to begin. He spoke for a long time about the old life of the Cherokee and how many were trying to keep their traditions alive.

Then he looked at Tyler and said, "We have a new member with us tonight and I hear he has a good story to tell us." There was a murmur of excitement. The Cherokee people loved a good story. "Tyler, Bear Killer, step forward and let us all enjoy your adventure."

Tyler was startled to hear his name being called and he looked at Walter with fear.

Walter whispered, "Do not be afraid, Tyler. You are among friends and they want you to feel at home, brother."

Tyler stood and walked forward. He began his tale in a quiet voice, but soon with the laughter and hoots he had to speak up. By the time he finished the people were shouting and whooping with joy.

Tyler finished by saying, "I really didn't have time to think about what I was doing. I am so happy that Walter found me and took care of me. He has taught me many new things that will stay with me forever. He has also given me many things to think about as I grow. He will always be my friend and brother. I want to thank all of you for your kindness and I am proud to have a little Cherokee blood in me. I will proudly tell anyone who asks that I am a Cherokee but I am also proud of the other heritages in me."

Ben came up to Tyler and put his hand on his shoulder.

"Bear Killer, you are my brother and your words have brought us laughter and joy! You fill me with pride to know you. Now, we will have many gifts for you in the coming days but we want to share this first gift with you tonight."

Ben took Tyler's shoulders and turned him to the left. Tyler looked across the fire and there stood his family. His mother, father, grandpa, two grandmas, his brother and sister and aunt and uncle all stood together with tears in their eyes. Tyler rushed to them and fell into their embraces.

The family spent three more days with the Cherokee people and all became a part of the gathering. Light Foot took Tyler's grandpa off on the second day and they spent the entire day in the forest, talking and laughing.

Promises were made to visit again and the family insisted that Walter make their homes a regular stop as he traveled around.

When the family was ready to leave, Tyler went to Walter and hugged him and said, "Walter, I want to thank you for all the gifts and bringing me out of the mountains. You have taught me many things that will stay with me, but more than anything else, you have given me much to think about. I have a good idea of who I am and where I come from, but thanks to you, I

Tyler Hill's Decision

think I know how to be a better person. You will always be my friend and I will try to make my family and you proud of me."

Walter said, "Tyler, my brother, we have given each other many gifts and I owe you much for giving me a chance to teach a young man some of the knowledge I have gathered in my many years. I am very proud of the young man you are and can see the man you will become. You will live in my heart."

The End